BRUNO LUMB

Published under licence by Brown Dog Books and
The Self-Publishing Partnership Ltd, 10b Greenway Farm, Bath Rd,
Wick, nr. Bath BS30 5RL, UK

www.selfpublishingpartnership.co.uk

ISBN printed book: 978-1-83952-849-1

Cover design by Andrew Prescott
Internal design by Andrew Easton

Printed and bound in the UK

This book is printed on FSC® certified paper

FSC
www.fsc.org

MIX
Paper | Supporting
responsible forestry
FSC® C013604

BRUNO LUMB

SON OF THE QUEEN OF BARDEZ

JENNIFER ELIZABETH LUMB

BROWN
DOG
BOOKS

This book is dedicated to Jenny, of whom there is only one.

"Love and Light"

GORAI

I think it must be Sunday. Why I say this is because everyone is running around with their shiny clothes on, including the men. Everyone loves shiny clothes for church: the women wear bright yellow satin skirts scattered with orange sunflowers and lime green leaves, and the men were wearing black shiny satin pants with three creases down the front. Apparently it was nothing to do with the fact that the wives had quickly ironed their trousers but the fact that each crease represented a holy spirit. The striped satin shirts that they wear are covered with polka dots of various sizes. Some women have little white hats on their heads trimmed with black laces and placed precariously just over one ear, with the other ear displaying a huge gold-plated earring made up of a circle of hoops that swung and sashayed in the Gorai Sea breeze. Some of the women have little pristine white gloves on their bird-like hands, and are carrying a little black book with them that has gold cross on the front. Nearly everybody has one with them, even the men apparently – they are called Bibles.

One by one they followed in an unbroken line, then climbed the white-limed steps into the white little house that I heard them call their church. I tried to follow them. Last Sunday I managed to get to the first line of seats when I was stepped on by a huge brute of a man in enormous black trousers with a Superman belt on that everybody was admiring. I

had never seen one of these belts before so I proposed that he must be somebody special by the adoration of the belt, but I later found out he was just an ordinary local with penchant for superiority and a pair of size ten plastic chappals that didn't match his gargantuan body. I squealed at the pain caused by this ugly hairy foot with ten dirty corns popping through various parts of the oily sandy chappals. They all noticed me squealing and limping as I tried to make a rocket exit through the brown double church door with the polished brass door knocker that was hanging on with one rusty nail – it was still swinging as banged my beautiful brown body on the escape gate. I slipped down the limed steps, which now seemed much higher than when I entered the church. I hopped over to a corner shared with two shabby dogs in the background.

The congregation was shouting at me to 'clear off, you idiot dog,' but I was only a one-month-old and it was very difficult for me to run with my paw broken in one thousand pieces. Oh yes, I've always been prone to exaggeration – that's my excuse, anyhow!

The two homeless dogs sat in the corner of the church, one beautiful mummy dog with shiny brown fur and one with scruffy-looking daddy dog. They beckoned me over to sit with them. I was a little nervous when I saw daddy dog's ear – it was full of crawling big fat creamy maggots, so I didn't sit next to him. I sat next to the pretty mummy dog, and she smiled at me and instantly I became her surrogate and handsome son. I was safe and sound now between the two amazing and most wonderful parents l could ever wish for. I really don't know where I came from, I think I just appeared from another mother's womb and after three

weeks was told to leave the pack and look after myself, and two weeks later here I am in the local church with a brand-new mummy and daddy and I was feeling very happy, especially when we had our supper – a communal wafer straight off the golden plate. I think Sunday is a very lucky day for me. My new mama gathered together in the little corner a pile of nice fishy bones straight from the Arabian sea and a dried blue bread crust dropped by big shiny crows. Every day seems like Sunday but I was happy with their offering. Sometimes I was lucky enough to find some little pools of water in little coconut shells they were very rough on my little black lips, but which matched my perfectly formed paws, except the baby paw which had just been crushed by the local stone crusher with the Superman's belt.

I settled in nicely with my most wonderful surrogate family in this whole wide world – never mind the universe or the black big hole that existed in the universe.

I think I'm happy! Yes, I'm very happy!

We all snuggled together in this holy family unit, but I was totally uneasy when I could see these greasy, plump, creamy maggots heading for the top of my immaculate head – after all, we were sitting by the priest's room hoping for the priest's blessed white wafers from the shiny golden plate The glare from the sun's rays made everything shine, including the holy group which was me, Mama and Papa.

After a long snuggly sleep, I was told to wake up by a lovely, warm, wet pink tongue – it was my most beautiful and caring and perfectly formed mother. I never knew what that word meant until today. Mother. But she insists on me calling her 'Mama'!

Perhaps she is from royalty as well as me. I always thought I was extra special, my head told me so, but for what reason? But at that moment I understood Mama is someone who loves and cares for you and helps you in everything, no matter how difficult. Truly I was a very lucky pup, born on the beaches of Gorai, which was near the Mumbai coastline.

So, the order of the afternoon was to visit several neighbours for alms, or so Mama explained to me – food from friends. So slowly we walked together by the sea, by the little white church, with me in the middle of

Mama and Papa. My feet were starting to burn in the hot sand, but Mama told me not to worry as we are nearly there.

'Where is nearly there?' I asked Mama.

'Oh, nearly there is the white house on the corner facing the church.'

I was hoping my feet would take me there without burning, so I ran ahead of them both and tumbled down a little ditch. Mama and Papa started laughing at me, so I waited for them. All together we climbed the only step belonging to this little white house. The sun over the years had bleached the white paint, revealing a blue underlayer which looked rather different to the pristine church where we had slept overnight. Handsome, scruffy daddy dog made his way to the front of the group and banged on the blue painted door. His black nails looking like shiny ember wood. Once more he banged with reverence, remembering the close proximity of the church and the priest.

Within seconds the door was opened – we all stood backwards a step when we saw the figure at the door. Both Papa and Mama offered a smile to this giant, and Papa offered his paw. Mama smiled at him and nodded her head from side to side. I stood like stone in the middle of an earthquake. My terror was unleashing at the picture of the person looming over head of me. IT WAS SUPERMAN! He had the sandy oiled chappals that covered the hairy, corned and dirty feet somehow. I couldn't look beyond his Superman's belt. I crept under Mama's cuddly legs for comfort when I heard this growly screeching voice playing the role of an actor. He made a flamboyant curtsey, throwing his arms down and sweeping the floor in a big bow. In doing so, he revealed a voluminous head of jet-black curls and roared to the three of us, 'Oh so! You have come for dinner. And who is this little chap in the middle. I suppose you to have come with them?'

But obviously I couldn't answer him. I was only a little four-week-old, and my knowledge of Marathi was non-existent. Mama whispered to me, 'Don't worry, I know he is fond of us; he calls us his creatures and he often gives us the leftovers of his fish curry.' I now know that the pieces of the leftover fish curry belonged to the leftover bones. But of course the bones had no spicy red curry paste on which I later acquired a taste for along with other royal food like roasted chicken with yummy crispy roast potatoes and Maggi chicken gravy that usually came on Sunday. I was told that it was customary in some countries to eat roasted chicken on a Sunday after church, and listen to family favourites on a radio. I already knew what a radio was because the beach shopkeeper played it all day long while drinking toddy with his friends. And if they had plenty of toddy, which looks like watery milk, then they were all happy telling jokes. I would also get all the leftovers of the crispy prawns and egg-fried rice.

At four weeks old I was catching up quickly – I knew who to smile at and who to sashay to and who to hide from. There was one small, skinny girl with black frizzy, curly hair who would charge at me with her long fork and try to eat my face. Mama was always telling me I had a face that was lovely enough to eat, but I didn't know what she meant by 'face'. I would always make a quick exit when I noticed the girl's knobbly knees running towards me. I don't know who she belonged to but her manners and eating habits were terrible.

I learnt that she belonged to nobody and came out of somebody's womb sockless but with a pair of mermaid shorts and a shiny big fork with a pink plastic handle that looked like it had been nibbled at with some sharp needle-like teeth. Not my teeth of course! I had much more manners than that – I hadn't been taught at all, but I had acquired them from my head. My head always told me how to behave and what to do. Lucky for me the toddy drinkers didn't like her either, and yelled at her to go back to where she came from!

'I don't know where I've come from,' she stuttered loudly. 'I know I came on a bus, with eight red wheels with Mr Potter.'

Mr Potter owned the local grocery shop, which sold rice and flour and sugar and tea and oil. Oh, and I forgot to say about the little packets of tiger biscuits that only cost five rupees a packet and tasted yummy!

I did not go there much because there was nothing interesting in there and no one ever offered a titbit of even a half a biscuit, so I saved my charm and wit for people who were deserving of some so I never really went hungry. Mama said I was one of the bonniest little things she had ever seen. Perhaps Mama was from Celtic ancestry? Of course I knew nothing of this Celtic ancestral talk, it was only years later when Elizabeth, the Queen of Bardez, and I would have lengthy chats at the pool when we became close buddy partners.

I followed her everywhere; she was my only sense of inspiration. I adored her and she adored me.

Meanwhile, Gorai was to be my home for a few more days. Little did I know what the future had for me – no beautiful little four-week-old, even with the imagination of a playwright, could ever imagine what would become of a little baby dog with a jet-black snout and a jet black stripe, I believe down my back. I don't know what a stripe is because I have never seen my back, only my beautiful mama has ever seen it when she was giving me a kiss and a slurp bath each evening before my sleep. She never did this for Papa – I think she feared the ever-roaming maggots from poor Papa's ears. He never complained about his hitchhikers but we could both tell by his nodding and shaking of his head that they bothered him. If we had fingers we could help!

Mr Superman would sometimes help him by burning the dangling mites with the end of his Woodbines. I thought Woodbines were some sort of food which you ate by sticking them to your bottom lip and making loud AAAHH! noises. Gradually they disappeared and all that was left was a bright red dusty end, and he would try to stick it on the head of one of these lazy fat maggots.

Sometimes you would hear a hissing sound and what I think was a cry for help to his unknown mother or father to come to its aid, but of course no help would come. I think the mothers and fathers had all escaped on the bus with eight red wheels.

Then after seconds of burning a big fat maggot it would fall off the brown woolly ear and land on the blue ceramic tiled floor that matched the hint of the blue painted door.

Superman was a super cleaner, because within a split second of this unbelievable televised happening, which we all three of us witnessed, the fat, slightly charcoaled, scaling creamy maggot was being blended to a soapy bliss, pulped by a sized ten plastic chappal and blended into the blue ceramic tiles like customised wax spray meant for Indian teakwood chairs, and within seconds had taken on an even shinier hue than before.

I think he would need at least three hundred of these creatures for his blue ceramic floor. It's a good job that Papa is a semi-resident!

The next morning there was something happening that was not normal for the Superman's house – Mr Superman had washed his face!

We all looked at one another in a somewhat fizzled, hysterical type of amazingness. The washing of the faces had rarely been witnessed in the nearly blue house – only once for a wedding and once for the funeral. Just as we were discussing the matter, a big bang of tin came on the front door that meant that his friend had come from Malad in Mumbai.

Then the little bony wrist appeared that belonged to Ritchie, the 'Encyclopaedia man,' who was Superman's friend. He was called this because of his unchallengeable knowledge that was packed into his tiny head. Ritchie knew and could answer any question asked on each and every subject, and never swaying on any answer he impressed each and every person who came across him. He was legendary, and part of folk law in Gorai. Much like Superman, with black curly hair and the curly haired toed feet – almost like twins, but one with brains and the other with wit and corns on his toes.

ENCYCLOPAEDIA MAN

They were not of Hindu culture but revered just as much. Ritchie bred and reared pigs, but one day when an order had come for a huge pig, both had forgotten how to process the order because of their whisky drinking (which was another pointer of their celebrity status). Neither could ever think how to start, so Superman, with the help of his khaki green underpants and a large not-so-shiny knife, jumped on the giant pig's back and rodeoed around the compound to the shrieking of the drunken crowd. After a few seconds the poor giant pig fell to the floor, either overcome by the weight of the Superman or his whisky-fumed breath or the not-so-shiny knife.

Nobody asked about his ending but left Mr Superman butchering the poor chubby pig into what he thought were butcher's terms like shoulder or hind or loin. His tale was as much preached as the story of the black book with the golden cross. But every day when the audiences were around with their whisky, which came from a glass bottle not a golden chalice, the same story came out from two pairs of hairy lips landing infectiously onto the crowd of innocent brains that were waiting for their enlightenment from the two famous Gorai born and bred whisky drinkers and storytellers.

They all drank and ate till their appetites were fulfilled, and after supper Superman would play his party piece which was to pick out the last fishbone from his plastic tooth that he stuck in his gum with Fevibond, a glue so famous it was reputed to be as strong as building cement but more pliable (it even worked on wet days). The Fevibond plug would be remoulded into the shape of a small grape, but white in colour, and pushed back into the cavernous hole where it would quietly sit until the next challenge of either sardine or local crab. It always did a marvellous job and was much cheaper than even a visit to the street dentist, who was a Mumbai version of Mother Teresa.

Adorned with the large rubber apron and a set of knives and pliers, the dentist would pull out a dishful of teeth, all without painkillers but often with mouthful of local brew. Superman's method was much simpler and luckily most of the remaining teeth appeared strong and superbly white. Apparently he could chew and macerate the whole chicken carcass while his dogs waited patiently for a scrap. Personally I have never witnessed this part of the folklore – it's only transcribed to me by his two part-time mutts, my papa and beautiful mama.

Superman walked to the door with Mr Encyclopaedia and we all followed in line. The hinge of the door was thumped shut by the large spade-like hand of Superman. Mama and Papa were looking very bewildered. I was picked up by the scruff of my neck and put in a red nylon bag and given to Ritchie. By this time both Mama and Papa had worked themselves into a state of mutt frenzy, jumping and barking at Superman and pulling on the hem of his shiny church trousers.

'OK, OK, you two mutts, it's OK! He is coming with us to Bastora, a little village in north Goa. We are going to see the Queen. He will be happy there; I can't afford to feed the three of you. You two have to guard the house.'

Suddenly the bread boy pushed his bike to where Superman was standing: 'I'm going away for a week. Simon, please leave two pao (Goan bread) each morning for these mutts here and get some cream from the vets for Scotties ears – and don't forget, because I'll be back soon and I don't want to see two starved mutts on my steps. Do you hear me?' A nod from Simon's head satisfied the grumbled Superman.

Mama was jumping in circles, having palpitations – this was the last few moments with her son. Even Superman realised the close bond that had formed between us all and tried to subdue Mama with a heavy clod on the top of her regal head, which was semblance of his affection.

From this very moment my whole world would change, but in what way? I don't know! I could never begin to imagine, and I knew in that present moment that I was frightened and confused and longing for Mama's warm body that she would give me as we fell asleep in our corner, that was covered in Mumbai newspaper that was there for our convenience. But of course we were too well educated and sensitive to use them, we would patiently wait until our benefactor would wake up and let us out. This was a nightmare, a bad dream, I was later told by Mama. Both Mama and Papa followed the two superheroes to the ferry boats. I knew nothing of this because I was encased inside the red nylon bag with long narrow handles. I whimpered at first but realised that I was only upsetting Mama more and more so had decided to be quiet and try to stop Mama's protests.

Now Mama and Papa's understanding had begun to accept the situation, so on this Thursday morning all our world had shattered and was completely out of our control. l could feel one last jump on Superman's trousers, one last attempt by my Mama to stop this atrocity that was thrust upon us.

Superman had become bad tempered with our behaviour and tried to kick Mama far away down the quayside where the queue was forming to board the ferry to the mainland, but luckily for her she had anticipated his move and scarpered quickly from between his legs to the safety of Papa, who was walking a few metres away from all these horrible theatricals.

They all boarded the ferry along with me in the red nylon bag. I could

hear Mama howl at the realisation that her new son was torn from her care. Papa growled a gentle growl of acceptance to my Mama there was nothing else that he could do. We were only here because of Superman's kindness in the first place, so perhaps things would be all right in the end.

I tried to fall asleep in the bag but the water from the ferry's seat was seeping into the nylon bag and my lovely brown fur was becoming cold with the salty water. This journey was becoming very worrying for me, encased in this dark red tomb with no Mama or Papa to reassure me.

I didn't have a chance to glance at my parents departure, but even the red nylon shopping bag didn't stop the lingering whimpers of my loving parents. As the ferry started moving I could hear somebody speaking with Superman, telling him that the dogs were still watching the boat's departure, and then said to Ritchie, 'I hope that bloody Simon doesn't forget the cream for Papa's ears.'

I was shocked. He never showed any sense of compassion for any animals before, he obviously keeps his feelings at arm's length, and whisky and bidis seem to do the jobs nicely. And honestly speaking I have only met him yesterday and today is only 11 am and too early for the whisky.

But, hey! What are these glass bottles that I have just weed on? That was meant for the outside road of the little blue house just thirty metres from the little white church, which I feel I will never see again.

Thoughts of Mama and Papa on the ferry side are on my whimpering mind. 'Please God always take care of them, I will be a good boy to whoever I'm going to. If God you only look after my Mama and Papa I promise I will be good for ever. AMEN!' I heard this word in the church – this must be a very important word because everyone said this very loudly and together. AMEN. AMEN.

Very quickly we alighted from the ferry, and, by rickshaw I believe, we went to the highway to catch the bus. Ritchie said dogs were not allowed on the coaches. Superman sputtered: 'Oh no! what can we do?' I shook next to the bottle of whisky, and worried – what is going to happen to me now? 'Don't worry,' said Superman to Ritchie, 'I brought a towel, he can hide in there. Luckily I have cups as well, so we can have our whisky and

The Rickshaw Ride from Gorai to the coach

21

he can sleep on my knees, wrapped in the towel, and we will sleep when we reach our first stop.'

Hurriedly I followed Superman's unspoken instructions to me and fell asleep in the kitchen towel. Well, actually it was an everything towel, a hand towel, kitchen towel, ash tray wiping towel, but it didn't matter to me. All the aromas landed into one big musty smell. Notice I never said bath towel? Superman believed that the body was self-cleansing and that was all there was to say about it.

We beach doggies used to love swimming in the surf, and luckily it kept us free from ticks and fleas. But I don't know about Papa's maggot ears – perhaps the salt water stung too much for my sensitive Papa to swim in the sea.

So now it was drinking time, a huge hairy spade with hairy fingers pushed me to one side of the red nylon bag and fumbled for the whisky bottle and two plastic cups. If you're thinking I'm far too wise and outspoken with all these terms of knowledge – plastic cups and whisky bottles and the words – for a five-week-old beautiful puppy, may I tell you that I'm writing these memoirs after ten full years, with my then-to-be-introduced benefactor, Elizabeth (the Queen of Bardez).

I always detected a robust sound of black satire and sarcasm when I heard them both speaking of her. But somehow, I knew that this person was to be someone special and this turned out to be most definitely true.

After what seems days, I could not hold my wee-wee any longer! Warm, golden liquid ran into to the all-purpose towel that I was wrapped in. It soaked into Superman's trousers, but because of the shiny material it ran like several rivers down his thighs and over his knees and down to his legs, finally swilling like a whirlpool onto Superman's plastic chappalled feet. 'What the hell is this, you ungrateful little bugger, you are pissing all over me!'

I didn't know who 'bugger' was – surly he didn't mean Ritchie? Even though he was a pig farmer I'm sure he was too much of a gentleman to piss on Superman's trousers. After a minute of calculation and reasoning I realised that the pisser must be me! I was thrown to the floor and left to look after myself.

I decided to fall asleep after some time on the welcoming warm towel that smelled of orchids and roses from my royal wee-wee. This journey, the first of my little life, was dreadful. Every second we seemed to be screeching around a sharp corner, and my thoughts wandered off to Mama and Papa. And although it made me sad it was better than my situation, not knowing what was to become of me, and somehow to surviving this nerve-shattering journey to somewhere, to see some person, in some small village in North Goa…

When I woke up, the sun was up to, and so to avoid trauma of the river ways I decided to look for a place for wee-wee, somewhere in secrecy where I wouldn't cause a problem. I toddled down the aisle and in-between the crowded seats until I found an empty spot by the bus steps where I could accomplish my little plan. Ooh, such happiness! I can't describe the feeling, which is very difficult for me now to put into words – the simpleness of my happiness as I shuffled to the floor, which was only three inches or more. Don't forget I was a baby then, and my little legs couldn't perform a daddy dog lift when he wanted to wee-wee – his wee-wee was stupendous, and it fountained into a glorious loop before falling onto the blue door at Superman's house where he functioned before meeting Superman two years ago.

I saw this several times and it was the only place he would carry out his ablutions. I tried to copy his but fell over on my three little legs, so I decided I would not bother again and just copied my longed-for Mama's wee-wee. It cascaded down all four steps of the bus. The pool was lustrous and gently warm, and I'm sure that this must be helpful to someone, perhaps the stream of soldier ants or the crackly shiny big black cockroach I spied in one of the plastic cups before I toddled off on my journey.

The bus from GORAI to Mapsua

The Rat Family Going to Gorai

Folks gradually awakened on the travelling bus and everyone started stretching and yawning, when all of a sudden, a huge greyness fell upon the bus. Superman had just stood up and stretched his arms out, touching the ceiling of the bus and breaking out into a huge yawn. His frightening statue had blocked out the eastern sun and the bus fell into an eclipse for a few bewildering seconds.

'Hey, Ritchie! Where's that little bugger? He is not here! We will get into trouble when the driver finds out'. Richie immediately jumped to attention and rearranged his red Ralph Lauren sports hat to the correct angle. Everything had to be perfect for Ritchie. I didn't realise that Ralph and Ritchie are the same name, but I had noticed that lots of boys and men were called Ralph, as they also had these hats, especially on the beach of Gorai. In fact I recollect Superman wearing a white one that only just fitted on top of his huge head that was covered in thick black curls that was smothered with red curry paste from his oily fish hand. I thought it must be Ritchie's hat because of the diminutive sizing of the

Superman's head but then realised that was the huge head of Superman that was at fault.

'For God's sake, man, help me find the little bugger!' It was then I realised that the little bugger was me, and to say I was perturbed at this statement was to say the least, but Superman has never been angry or violent with me, so I wasn't too worried. I glanced from behind the driver's seat and I witnessed two objects: one diminutive with a red and grey T-shirt that meticulously matched his red Ralph Lauren baseball cap, which was adjusted every two seconds, and a rhinoceros-sized figure with a camouflage shirt that wasn't working at all in the aisles of the bus. Both were on all fours and travelling in the opposite direction, looking beneath the seats and on people's bags and sheets and shouting no name as such, because I have not been christened. 'Come, boy,' they shouted in disguised voices, 'Come, boy, come, boy,' again and again. This remarkable displacement of emotive actions were arousing many of the passengers, some intending to find out the reason for this early-morning theatre. 'Ooh, we have lost something – nothing much but we have to find it. We think it had rolled down the bus.' Which in fact I had done!

I had rolled all over the bus but because I found nothing interesting I carried on my rolling journey until I found the perfect place – the bus stairwell! The driver's eyes were steadfastly on the road so he didn't spot my 'little bundle of joy,' or as the bus company would call it, 'unwanted cargo'. Suddenly I felt so sorry for myself, and great big hot and wet crocodile tears came rolling down my velvety soft fur and dropped into the crevice of my delicate baby mouth to remind me that it could be breakfast time soon. Lifting my perfectly formed baby head I noticed Ritchie stroking his dark brown hair. His quiet beautiful eyes popped out of his exquisite face: 'He is here, Baba, here is here – the bugger is here.'

I knew who the bugger was, but this 'Baba' person? I had no idea who he was talking to. 'Oh my God, thank the Lord for that,' I heard Superman's voice bellow out loud. It was then that I realised that Superman was in fact called Baba. I was later to find out that Superman in fact thought of himself as a Baba, as a spiritual and holy person, but I was still even years later unable to fit the two together. A nervous twitch came to my face as I trotted to meet Ralph (Ritchie). His bony, veined hand reached out and grabbed me behind my neck, and before I knew it I was securely fitted under Ralph's new red-and-grey striped shirt and whisked back to the safety of the red nylon carrier bag. The all-purpose orchid and rose scented towel was thrust over my head as I descended into the bag with the couldn't-care-less attitude of the fish seller dumping their mackerel into someone's dirty shopping bag.

So, I suppose that means no breakfast for me, 1 thought, trembling. I quietly went to rest and awaited my fate. After the almighty shouting of sweaty sleeping bodies, we came to the step where I had for over five hours been depositing my 'sweet smelling wee–wee,' as Mama would call it. I can't understand because I have not drunk any water and just eaten the bottom of the McDonald bun and some cheese and onion crisps that had been shaken all over my velvety head and rested in my blue nylon collar, and some from Ralph that had been politely placed in front of me on a white paper plate.

I forgot to tell you that my fur was a beautiful brown-red colour. I heard Mama once say that my fur was auburn and I possibly could be from a Celtic clan like her. My snout was black and so were my perfectly draped ears. Apparently, according to Mama, dogs with pointed-up ears were a lower class of country dogs.

I was very happy with her rendition, but even before her amazing motherly remark I always knew in my head that there was something very special about me – in one year to come I would find out just how remarkable I actually was. Sprinkly, oily, wee-wee adorned many of the passenger's legs as they thumped their big dirty nailed feet into the large pool of my flowing sweet-smelling unwanted bodily fluids. Mama had taught me all of the Celtic terms of body etiquette, bodily fluids both numbers one and two, which luckily I didn't need to perform, because the red big bus had no little patches of grass for baby dogs. In fact it had no patches of grass for the big people in the whole big journey. There was only two stops which I heard the driver call, 'This is your relieving and food stop.' So that's where the bun and the crisps came from – perhaps I'll find another scrap of crisps under the seat when Ralph puts me down? Unfortunately Ralph put me straight into the red carrier bag. Something was about to happen, and I was right – we were pushed into the sweaty queues by the holy Baba, followed by Ralph and the red nylon bag, which was clutched to his non-sweaty new striped shirt. I didn't feel too safe in the red nylon bag because when Baba was pushed back by the swaying crowd into the Ralph's steely chest, I felt I was being pounded in a spice crusher with a marble pestle.

With one last push, Baba landed to the last step of the bus and his

cheap, one hundred rupees plastic chappal gave way on his left foot and he went flying into a yellow plastic waste paper dustbin. The camouflage shirt tucked itself into the bottom part of the bin while Baba's shiny pants were suitably resting into the bottom half of the bin. I was comatose with my wee-wee and waiting for help, which took a long time to arrive, people in India are not very quick to help people in distress (or upturned into the yellow waste bin).

So Ralph, after a cautionary moment of thought, stepped forwards and thankfully placed me on the floor where I remained both silent and motionless for what seemed an eternity.

Ralph pulled Baba's shiny trousers, which were a bit wet with some sweet-smelling nectar, but nothing was happening. It was decided by the crowd that the waste bin should be rolled over to the sandy floor, where Baba could use his one remaining chappal as a leverage to push himself out of his colourful coffin, accompanied by roars of laughter as Baba's other chappal fell upon foreign ground. I tried to listen to Ralph's roars,

BABU HAVING BEEN RESCUED FROM THE BIN

but I was never to hear one that meant Ralph was a man of uttermost respect, I can honestly state.

As three burley Goans helped with the Gorai colourful coffin situation, Baba was pulled to safety by the new anointed St Ralph. Baba lifted himself to his knees with packets of cigarettes used as an ash tray and grained ash trickling down his beautiful hair, and a plastic tray with dripping sachets of tomato sauce adorning his army camouflaged shirt which from a distance now looked like summertime roses sitting on the branches.

'The king of Gorai has risen from the death!' I heard the anointed one say. I must say that the king of Gorai had taken it very well until I heard him shout at the bus driver in an unknown language to me. But I believe from another source that he was going to sue the bus company for physical damage for both body and Sunday clothes and for him stepping on the bottom step of Mountain Dew which obviously should not have been there (Mountain Dew is a very popular drink in India – it tastes delicious and is similar colour to my number ones and apparently tastes divine).

WHATS HAPPENED TO BABA !!!

The bus driver just shook his head in utter oblivion and gestured silently in a curled-up fist for him to move on. Baba, Ralph and the red nylon carrier bag carried out that request, and moved on. After Baba had composed himself we boarded a black-and-yellow rickshaw, and after bargaining a price of one hundred rupees we set off on a new adventure to the Queen of the Bardez' house. It was still in monsoon time and the rain was heavy and hot after leaving the bus station. At around 6 am we were at our new destination.

PIARA

In the village of Bastora there was no one to be seen, the village was human-less, totally different to the ferry junction of Gorai. Baba took out his shiny black Nokia mobile phone and rang for the Queen to tell of our arrival. The rickshaw man, after seeing the house, left wishing he had asked for more money. We had arrived at the most beautiful house that I had ever seen, and I couldn't imagine Baba ever knowing some queenly person that belonged to this heavenly abode. The mansion was

MY NEW HOUSE "PIARA"

called Piara, which I heard them both laugh at such a prosperous name! All l could do as a little nothing was pack away into my sweet little brain a wonderful picture of unimagined mystical beauty. Piara in Hindi meant 'the loved one'.

Piara's boundary wall was painted creamy pale pink, almost ice-cream colour, and had a huge ten-foot-tall gate adorned with flamingos, their eyes filled with emerald gems. This must be an animal lover, I thought, so perhaps the Queen could begin to love me? After all this was the purpose of a 600-kilometre trip to find me a permanent home away from the turmoil of the blue paint splashed everywhere. I noticed first that Piara had none of that careless attitude of Gorai. No splashes of pink or cream paint to be viewed anywhere. This home was owned by someone with style and attitude, and when I saw her for the first time I fell in love. But firstly Baba and Ralph had to climb Mount Everest – the brown-painted gate adorned with flamingos.

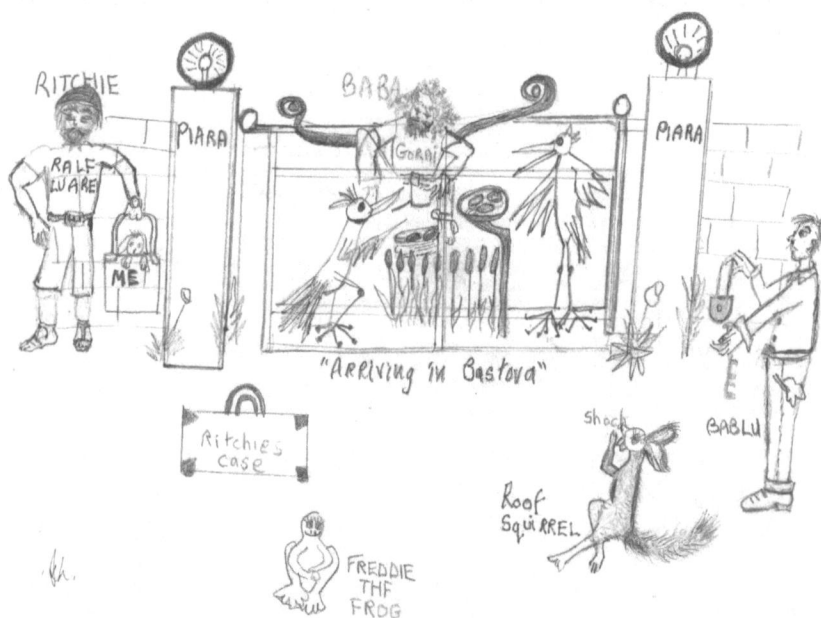

"Arriving in Bastora"

Ralph held the red carrier bag with me trembling inside. Baba scaled the gate alone; his eighteen-stone body was searching for footholds in the gate but the gaps were too small for a size-twelve foot. He decided to free his feet of the rubber chappal that was hampering his journey on Everest. Finally he had scaled the top, and his chunky frame sat precariously on the top of the gate. Nervously he threw over his gargantuan leg, and, drenched in Goan rain, began his trip over the summit to the other side. Baba's beautiful jet black curly hair had stretched with warm rain and blocked his view. Two bucket-sized hands swept the sticky curls apart and he stumbled slightly on the mossy Jodhpur stone, and now it was Ralph's turn as he passed the red nylon bag through the gates along with Ralph's outdated computer case which he treasured above anything.

The Queen stood on the step of her pale pink marble veranda looking astonishingly regal in her silk kimono embroidered with silken threads and luminescent pink pearls. In my short five weeks of life I had never seen such a vision, it was almost like the mother Mary in the little white church, near the almost blue painted house in Gorai, and to this day I have never witnessed such a sight to behold and hopefully she will become my benefactor in the years to come.

Ralph and Baba had scaled Everest successfully and started to walk towards Mother Mary. 'You're early!' she shouted to them, 'I didn't expect you until 8 o' clock.'

'Yes! The bus driver was practising for the Grand Prix!' I have no idea what a Grand Prix was, but Ralph shouted to the Queen, 'You still look beautiful, even at this time of the morning!' Ralph was a bit of charmer, I believe – that was what Baba shouted to the veranda steps.

Baba excitedly told her that he had a gift for her. 'A gift?' she answered. 'You've never bought a gift for me as long as I've known you, what is it?' she jokingly retorted.

To which Baba replied, 'It's a dog.'

'A dog?' she replied, 'You know I don't like dogs – all that fur and licking all over the place.'

'Well if you don't like him I'll take him back to Gorai,' he answered. Lifting the red carrier bag he said, 'Here is the gift, I brought this dog all the way from Gorai for you.

There in Bastora, the next few words shattered my being. I started to shiver, my head was spinning and my heart was broken by these words. I will never forget, they were stamping on my little baby brain for the next few moments. 'OK, I'll think about it,' said the Bardez Queen, who I heard Baba call, 'Liz'.

I'm an orphan, I thought, a child of the unwanted, the last unpicked strawberry from a dried-up strawberry patch. The Bardez queen was to be my benefactor for the future. I would never get back to Gorai by myself, to see my adopted parents again. I tried to cry for some semblance of pity, but the tears had dried upon the route to my heart. So this is it, is it? The insides of the red carrier bag were to be my fate forever.

I popped my head to the top of the carrier bag. Slowly I lifted my crouched head and when I saw the softness of her mouth break into a genuine smile I think she was quite impressed by my little goatee beard. 'Ooh! He looks like a little Chinese man with those whiskers, let me lift him out.'

Luckily I hadn't done a wee-wee, so I smelt quite fresh. I know she was impressed by the softness of my fur because she gently put me against her cheek to feel my softness. I think I've won her over! She held me for some minutes. I had never been held like that ever and the softness of her head reminded me of Mama in Gorai but her smell was of rose petals and her skin of silk. Mama came second in line now, oh what a fickle little character I had become! But that's what happens when you are without love and without a home and someone to love you. I hope she loved me for the days to come as I had said before.

'Don't worry,' retorted Baba, 'I will take him back if you don't like him.'

So, it was decided upon that I would be here on a trial period and to see if I would win a place in the Queen of Bardez's heart.

Ralph opened his mouth for the first time, 'He will be good company for you, Liz. He is a nice little chap and no bother at all.'

The Queen nodded her head to Ralph and said, 'Let's see.'

So here I am for a trial period of seven days, so I had better be on my best behaviour – no wee-wee or poo in the house. I hope she has newspapers for that, for that was what I was used to in Baba's house, because at the moment I couldn't make it to the outside of the garden because to every door there were at least nine steps and I know that I will not manage the depth of the steps. The only steps I had experienced before were the steps at the little white church and I only managed those because the centres of the stairs were well worn.

Gently my new mama placed me on a very slippery floor, my little leg slipping in opposite directions for a moment. I hope the rest of the floors are not like this, I thought. Of course, they were, but by the time I had reached the kitchen I had mastered the art of tiny little cautious steps. Soon it will become like second nature to me. All three of them laughed at me – that was a good sign, as laughing means approval. Good! I'm doing well in the human physiology part of it, let's hope I pass the seven days approval test and perhaps I'll get a silver star that I sometimes see on school children's jumpers.

'What do I feed him?' the Queen anxiously asked Baba. 'Oh anything you've got – leftover bread or yesterday's rice…' I must have looked pretty miserable on hearing that sentence because my hopefully new mama's voice became a little angry. 'Would you like to have dried-up rice or stale bread? No, you wouldn't! I have some roasted beef – I'm sure he will love that.'

My mouth started to water and my little black tail rotated in a clockwise position. I'm in a Vastu house and from conversation I know clockwise

is the correct transition and anti-clockwise would mean I didn't like the statement. I don't know about beef, though! I'm looking forward to tasting it. If my new mama eats it then it means that it is manna from heaven.

Firstly Mama gave me a bowl of water from her water machine. Baba tried to interrupt by saying to her not to waste the filter water on the dog – tap water is all he is used to. I thought that was a very hurtful thing to say about me. After all, I was his newly adopted son and as yet I have no home and mostly no name. I don't like the 'bugger' name he calls me at all. The little bowl she laid down on the Jaisalmer floor, which sparkled with the light. 'Why have you given him a crystal bowl?' Baba said. 'Plastic is good enough for him.'

'I don't own anything plastic, Baba, and until I buy him a proper dog bowl then this will be sufficient.'

UNTIL I BUY HIM A PROPER DOG BOWL! Oh, oh! My little heart started to sing. That sounds like I have a big, big chance of this becoming my home. Perhaps the seven-day approval has already finished, but I mustn't be too presumptuous – best behaviour is the must of the day.

My drinking bowl was almost as big as me, if fact it wasn't a bowl it was a tea saucer. I believe my little head would have trouble reaching the top of the bowl, the water was fresh and tasty and with no floating mosquitos and flies or no floating dog-ends that often floated into my dog dish. How different this house was. I was horrified when I first heard the word dog-ends. I truly thought that they were the bottom of dogs, then Mama lifted from a large silver cabinet a piece of brown something or the other which Mama called beef. One day I saw a dog-end hanging from Baba's mouth, and in my little mind I thought of him eating a dog and now that poor little dog was hanging from Baba's lips issuing clouds of smoke – I had never heard or nor seen such a thing.

Meanwhile, Mama was cutting the beef in small slices that were robbed by Baba before they reach my little porcelain plate that was covered in yellow daffodils and rendered with poet William Wordsworth. That was all about the love of the 'said flowers'. I have to remind you that this point I seem to be a clever little dog, too clever to be born at a fishing village, but this knowledge I acquired over the next few months and years... Oops! I've let it out of the bag! Yes, Mama did adopt this 'poor little son of Gorai!' I didn't want to tell you so soon but now I have told you now, so I'll carry it on.

I was reading the poem of Wordsworth on the saucer between the slices of the beef placed on the saucer. The saucer kept spinning round and I was getting another neither a piece of beef or reading some words to make me happy. So I decided to stop and focus on how to attain the beef from the spinning saucer. The answer was to keep my left paw on the side of the porcelain saucer.

Before Baba and Ralph could devour the plate of beef that was destined for yours truly, Mama shouted at them and said the remainder of the beef was for her son. Wow, now I'm her son! I couldn't believe it. I gulped the water so quickly I started to choke by the end of it. Smoke was bellowing from Baba's hairy nostril and swilling above his black curly hair. I wondered who that dog had been – at least it wasn't Mama or Papa or me, but I would have been a very tiny dog-end.

I realised that I was dreaming with happiness: her son! l could hardly breath with excitement and the water that was enveloping my baby throat. Quickly she picked me up and placed me over her shoulder and for some reason patted my head. I calmed down and the hiccups vanished. We walked some steps around the veranda, with me on her shoulders. I noticed her pink nails were the same colour as mine – our hair almost the same. 'If he is your son,' retorted Baba, 'then you have to name him.'

'That's right,' she replied, 'let's think what it should be, OK? I always loved the name Bruno. One of my friends I was very fond of was called Bruno and I intend to love my second Bruno just as him.'

Suddenly I felt as if I had been awarded a gold cross and a diamond crown. I was loved without doubts, and by a woman with great beauty and esteem – this was one of the greatest days of my life. I think it was because I visited the little white church with the little cement steps that I had been blessed beyond my imagination! Oh how happy I am, if only Mama and Papa were with me, but I mustn't ask for more as that would be rude and ungrateful. And now that God was always part of my life I'm sure that Mama and Papa would be safe with a new set of benefactors. The only thought on that was negative, because I know that baby pups were adopted rather than older dogs, which wasn't fair, because older dogs still need someone to love and look after them.

My first bite into the tiny slices of beef were beyond my imagination. The beef was succulent and tasty beyond belief. My head was swinging with happiness. I didn't want to eat them all it was my habit to leave some food until the evening, but today I didn't want to risk leaving anything for two reasons: I didn't want my new Mama to think I didn't like it, and I didn't want Baba to steal it. One time in Gorai he took a large fish bone I was saving for supper from my dirty paper food plate, he put it in his mouth, sucking every morsel of flesh meant for my beautiful little spiky teeth. At supper, for fifteen minutes, he chewed and then took it out of his mouth, and then picked his strong healthy white teeth until his front tooth came out. Spikes of blood trickled from his lower lips but he seemed unperturbed. Deftly he strode to the toolbox and opened the rusty iron lid and lifted out a small packet of white araldite, filled the tooth with glue and popped it into his bleeding gum. By then the bloody fat mackerel bone had been thrown into the greasy floor of the living room. I looked at it and thought to myself not to bother with supper tonight. Sometimes it's better not to know the history of one's food. I would be so thin and not a fluffy little ball if I had noticed this performance before so tomorrow's dried bread would be much appreciated – that's if the crows don't get it first. I just can't stand those crows; sometimes they are on patrol before daybreak and until sunset.

Anyhow, let's get back to Mama's first sign of love for me: clean clear water, juicy succulent beef served in style with crystal saucers and a porcelain plate. I much prefer Mama's style of eating and drinking and no oil spills on the floor to hamper my dainty little black feet. When I say black feet, I mean black fur not dirty feet for my new wonderful and adorable Mama. I would be licking myself clean after each meal.

Days never followed a pattern in this house of Mama's, but you could always rely on Baba's day of nothingness, as he would lie on bed like a big golden buddha just watching TV and eating each and everything he could think of that was in Mama's kitchen. To actually help in the house in anyway would never enter his mind.

Firstly, Mama would give me a plate of doggie biscuits and vegetables followed by a crystal-clear filtered water. I preferred it chilled from the giant silver cupboard which I now knew it to be called a fridge. Mama's was no ordinary house. Everywhere was picture perfect. Apparently, I hear in Ralph's conversation that Mama was an artistic genius not only in her design of fairy-tale wedding gowns but her ability to design each and every piece of furniture in each room. Even without inspecting the work-in-progress she would do intricate drawings detailing the colour of each piece. She knew the shape, colour and design of every unique piece of furniture she would have in her magnificent Portuguese mansion which was renovated with an immense love from a wreck of palace built in 1888. People would stop and stare at the house outside of the front wall. Piara was a true Diamond among a handful of nothingness.

Fitting into life at Piara would be no problem in my little life, I could never know how love could feel. Even Bablu, Mama's security guard, would carry me under his arm while sweeping the marble floor. He was an extremely educated man from Bengal. Tall, young and extremely handsome, and sometimes Mama would be frantically looking for me when I would be warmly snoozing under Bablu's loving armpit. So now I'm loved by two people it's making me so happy to be loved by them but I'll never forget my first love in Gorai, Mama and Papa who showed me the meaning of love. Without them I could be a shabby little street dog roaming the beaches of Gorai looking for someone to love and someone to feed me.

That day the rain poured and poured, making Ralph's hat fall further and further over his shining coconut-coloured head. What was to happen today, I thought? Was I to be left with Bablu or should I be going with Mama in the rickety dark blue Austin van belonging to Baba? Ralph opened the van door for Mama then Ralph got in the back of the van. What was to become of me? I'm known about the village now, and there could lurk around the gate someone who would like to steal me for their dog-ends or simply for my beauty. My little heart began to pound – what would they do to me? I didn't worry for long because Mama in her infinite wisdom had decided to climb into the back seat with my doggie basket – my Mama thinks of everything, I am so lucky. I don't even want to grow up into a big dog and lose my baby status – I love being loved.

So, where are we going today? My beautiful Mama stood still, her hair shined like golden honey in the noonday sun, and her gown sparkled with little fireworks of peachy thingamajigs. I do not know what they are called but her silk gown was on fire with these thousands of creatures that lived there, from top to bottom. I almost envy them. If I were a little peachy thingmajig I would be with Mama most of the day, but perhaps peachy thingamajigs have had every right to be near Mama for they knew her long before me. Mama once told me it was better to be giving to one's fellow friends than to have thoughts of evil, whatever that is; but I certainly knew what kindness was, as Mama had shown it to me since the first day she met me.

We drove into Mapusa some short distance away to buy some groceries, which included many bottles of rum (old monk rum) and bottles of beer both for Baba and Ralph. They both drank Kingfisher beer from noon and through the afternoon and evening the bottles of rum and coke. Every evening I sat beside Mama's side thinking of her only and thinking how lucky I was to be her son. I was truly blessed by that visit to the little white church with the slippery steps. It was worth that horrible fracture of my little left foot. Late on in the night other friends of Baba arrived and gathered around for their free drink of rum and freshly fried samosas. Mama said I was too young for that culinary delight, but I didn't mind because she had just broken a big succulent chicken leg into baby pieces with strict instructions for no one to touch it because this was her son's dinner.

When I had finished my succulent dinner I looked at her perfect face and lifted my paw into a 'namaste' thank you. With her rose-coloured smile she lifted me gently into her warm arms and I fell into a sleepy blissfulness. l don't know how long I was in heaven but when I awoke the dearest friends were already leaving so Mama placed me onto the grass for my nightly wee-wee. My little pink paw nail caught onto the families of peachy things and thousands upon thousands all tumbled to the ground of the pink marbled veranda – I was hopelessly upset because I know the peachy things go to bed early but what could I do? They all looked comfy, though, in the marble corner – a new colony of peachy things had joined our home.

Mama must have noticed my tiredness and gently lifted me in her arms and tickled my little black nose with her dainty loving fingers, and walked with me through the corridor until we reached the huge pink marbled bathroom where she wrapped me round and round in a big white fluffy towel. I looked like a baby rose in the centre of the towel.

Gently she wiped my nose and lips with a small towel that smelt of roses. She then gently placed me in the centre of the embroidered cushion which she had made for me. Slowly I watched her walk away from me and I became nervous of the situation. Was I to be left alone in the hugeness of her room? She stood upon her perched toes to reach the top cupboard and from within she brought a dainty silver box and lifted the lid slowly. She looked upon its contents and picked out a little silver necklet with a pink onyx heart hanging from the silver ring. She said it was the first little anklet she had ever bought, and the onyx heart was a symbol of love. It was a treasured piece of love and she was bestowing it upon her beloved son. Lovingly she placed it around my dainty neck, using the extension chain to make it fit perfectly. 'Hmm! I think my little son is putting on weight! Never mind it will last several more weeks and then we will have to make another one for you, Bruno.'

Gently she lifted me up to the mirror. Ooh! I looked like a king! I don't think I should venture to the gate anymore. It could spell out danger for

you are beautiful Bruno!

Madame admiring Bruno

me. Mama must have thought the same as she looked at our reflection and said sweetly, 'Bruno, my little king, you look so regal.'

My little heart was bursting with pride and joy for her. Still wrapped in white fluffy towel that smelled of roses she gently placed me on my embroidered bed and said a little prayer to her friend (God) and climbed into her huge cream and golden bed. She placed her sweet face on her silky cotton pillow cases and distributed her golden hair on the pillow to resemble the rays of the sun. 'Goodnight, my darling Bruno, I love you, my son! Sweet dreams.' My heart was longing to say the same to her, for I truly felt the same, but why could those words not come out from my trembling mouth?

Why were there these huge differences between humans and animals? I have often heard people say, 'Oh, they are only dumb animals. Is that what they think about us? In my heart and head I had so many loving words that I wish they had the courage to creep their way from my heart and head and meet halfway and express in real words that humans have and tell her the greatness of my love for her, for her generosity to each and every creature and even to the peachy things. She left the peachy thingamajigs on the marble veranda. Mama said, 'Leave them in peace. Poor things! They look pretty in the sun so I'm sure that they are happy and they seem to be great friends to the silver things on the golden gate.' Which of course they were. This veranda was where I first landed my little feet, it is truly place of magic.

In the morning I woke and tumbled from the bed still attached to the towel. I wanted to wee-wee but Mama was still sleeping, so I struggled to release my leg, which was exceedingly hard to say the least. But with the help of my front paw I finally struggled free after gaining my decorum. I uncrossed my back leg and daintily walked from her room. I was literally elated when I saw some newspaper placed near the courtyard door. Phew, thank goodness for that. Ooh! The bliss of that warm wee-wee. I crouched down on the newspaper and released my warm friend. Now I can relax, I thought to myself! Then I walked on the second paper to do my number two. This is so embarrassing. I tried to do it when no one was around like we were trained well at Baba's house. Mama was pleasantly surprised by my impeccable house habits. Soon I could hear Mama get out of her queen bed, and slowly she walked to the courtyard where she noticed Bablu picking the papers. 'Oh, is that Bruno's wee-wees?'

'Yes!' he replied, 'and his number two! He is such a clever little dog. He cautiously uses a clean paper for each.'

Mama replied, 'Oh, what a clever boy you are my son, not once have you messed the floor. Let's go for a little walk around the garden.'

We slowly walked to the garden and as we approached the steps Mama and Bablu almost fought to pick me up and carry me down the steps. Mama won!

Bablu was such a gentle soul and I know Mama was extremely fond of him, and he only worked at Piara so he could be always near her. Mama told me that he was without doubt the owner of an academic brain and a great lover of art. In my brain I visualised them always being together and eventually walking hand in hand into the sunset. But I don't know if this will ever happen. Daintily, Mama approached the steps while Bablu held her hand and together descended the steps together with me tucked in the middle under my Mama's arm.

A GIFT FROM THE
CHAMPA TREE

The garden was beautiful, with the morning sun flickering its long orange fingers over the branches and resting upon the crystal-clear pool water.

Each day we carried out the same routine. Occasionally Bablu's arm would rest on Mama's shoulder, pretending he was protecting her. Some of the pink Jodhpur stone had come out of place but Mama didn't mind. Mama once told me she didn't like everything perfect (I hope she's not including me in this). We would walk around the huge blue pool and admire each and every one of the garden trees. Mama showed me her favourite tree of all. Billow-mard. She didn't say it out loud for other trees to hear, for she loved them all and told me it had been scientifically proven that trees had human feelings too. When any tree was ill, they would talk to it and send food through their root system to make it well again. If only our society were the same, she would say, if people had love and compassion for one another then our life would be so wonderful.

We walked to the other side of the pool where another of Mama's favourite trees stood. It was a majestic Champa tree with a silver blue bark and large perfect flowers that looked like hand-carved porcelain, and was blessed a with musky fragrance. Mama told me that one day she was in the pool and daydreaming. She said she must have been some fifteen metres away from the tree when she noticed from the corner of her eye one of the Champa flowers had lifted itself from its branch and flew into the air to where Mama was stood. She said it was a magical moment because she was only thinking how the beautiful the tree was. When this miracle happened that day there wasn't even a breath of wind, the day was perfect, but the flower had flown over to her and landed one metre from Mama's body. Slowly she picked it up to her mouth and gently inhaled its perfume. 'You are beautiful,' she said to her new friend. Firstly Mama thought that it may have died and looked for the telltale sign around the edges of her petals, but the petals were perfect and the perfume exotic. This was no ordinary deciduous. But the petal had wanted to be in Mama's presence. Everyone loved Mama – there was a spiritual presence about her.

'Aah! I know what has happened to you. You wanted to be in my hair, didn't you? You are beautiful!' Carefully Mama tucked it behind several of her golden curls, the two curls looked serenely perfect with the flower tucked between them. And there it remained until nighttime when Mama would walk to her golden bed. But the flower was not ignored, she was placed on Mama's dressing table just one inch away from Mama's glorious bed.

'Bruno, go and do a wee-wee and then to bed.' I suddenly remembered I had no dinner, how could I tell her? I cuddled next to her silver nightgown and sashayed against her skin. I gently tugged at her gown and looked to her face. My diamond stream of tears gently touched her gown, 'Oh, what is it, Bruno? Your tears are so beautiful, but sad.'

'Madam, we have forgotten to feed him,' she heard Bablu say from the kitchen.

'Oh no! Silly Mama. I'm so sorry, my darling. Bring it here, Bablu, and I'll feed my little boy.'

Gently she lifted the juicy succulent pieces from the daffodils plate.

My heart rested in contentment as she broke creamy pieces of chicken into very delicate pieces. How could I ever think of her forgetting me? I scolded my brain to never let it happen again. My heart would never act in that manner. I told it sometimes it's good to remind people, or as in my case my brain is to be considerate before acting out of place.

'Please forgive me, Bruno, for forgetting your dinner,' she said. But there was no need for it. I understandably smiled at Mama because I instantly knew that Mama was always thinking of something else; trees and flowers and birds and animals in the garden. They all had temporarily stolen her away from me.

The Champa flower sent its fragrance from its petals to our bed sides, sending its love to our bed which we lovingly accepted. And after a short time we both drifted off into a long blissful sleep. The next morning woke us with the pouring rain banging on the roof. It was going to be a miserable day. So, goodness knows what we would do. Normally by now Bablu was sweeping the floor with me in his arms. He moved so slowly that I felt I was part of his soul. I never moved or swung to get down. I was perfectly happy tucked in his arm with the broom in the other arm and off I would fall into a lovely snooze again.

It was almost 1 pm when I heard Mama's cry that it would be time for lunch in half an hour. I wondered what it would be for lunch – my Mama would only eat fruit until the evening but I was to eat scrambled egg. Ralph and Superman ate food made by a fellow villager. Prawn thali pork shacuti, fish thali, rotis and beef curry and rice or any combination. Sometimes he would order for the whole day and by lunchtime it would have all gone. Mama wouldn't be bothered, and refused to order more. Greed is not acceptable in her book; if he was paying then it would be OK, but she certainly wouldn't, and this person certainly wasn't going to get his excessiveness granted. He could eat enough for eight people and drink as much as the world's ocean.

I'm two months old now. The Gorai guests have outstayed their welcome. Mama was getting tired of pandering to there every whim but she most of all hated the evening trips. She never liked to leave me, and Superman always seemed jealous that Mama wanted to decline his offer. Or was it that he just didn't want to pay for his evening out? I think Mama was becoming tired of them both. This particular day Mama decided to decline their offer so as soon as they left, Mama and I sneaked out to the pool, in the moonlight. You could see the fireflies darting up and down. I was fascinated by them and occasionally Mama's hair was entangled with the dragonflies' transparent blue wings.

BABLU

The shadow of the gnarled mango tree reflected its shape across the silver moon sky. This was a scene for writers to behold. In the distance we heard the subdued voice of Bablu. 'You're OK, Mam. They've gone out of the gate and Mr Kevin rudely told me to ask madam for courtesy tips.' 'The cheek of it!' Mama replied, and they both laughed loudly together and fleetingly held hands. 'We will be free of trouble this evening, in that case, Bablu. We can have our meal together on the veranda.'

I think the veranda is the most beautiful place in the whole house. From the apex of the veranda hung the most beautiful light fitting made of crystal and silver, which had an intricate pattern cut out all over it, which allowed the light bulbs to shine out of it as it were a moonbeam of flickering stars. The veranda windows were handmade and the panes were made up with beautiful pearlised oyster shell. The whole balcony was full of starlight. This exquisite, natural window you will rarely find in Gorai.

Bablu placed a little green marble table in the centre of the veranda. On it he placed two jade green crystal goblets and one little glass bowl, three large crystal plates with matching side plates and an array of silver cutlery and some starched white linen napkins. The two golden gates sparkled with little silver rays similar to the ones on Mama's robe. Everywhere seemed to be a ray of light and illumination.

Mama poured some light sparkling wine into the goblets and some sparkly water for me in my crystal dish, while Bablu served the roasted vegetables and succulent prawns into the crystal plates. My pieces of velvety chicken breast were arranged in perfect manner to complement the dancing daffodils. Bablu was visionary and romantic, the night needed no conversation, and I was happy sitting opposite with Bablu, mainly because in that position I could see all of my Mama's beauty. I was forgetting about my waiting chicken and was reminded by Mama with the sentence of, 'Do you have no appetite tonight, my darling Bruno? I don't think you have touched one morsel of your dinner.'

This evening I shook my head from my constant thought of what it would be like just Mama, Bablu and me, with the nod of my head and the smell of my supper. The thought just flew away with the nighttime fireflies.

Mama placed a little chilled water on my saucer. It was a perfect night while Mama and Bablu spoke about the poet Rabindranath Tagore, it seemed they spoke for hours of the love of the poet and the love of his writing. I just loved watching their faces. I didn't need my scrumptious food or to be caressed by a silken hand. Just the echoing of their happiness was all I needed.

The shifting of the moon reminded us of the time we were so engrossed with one another's presence, but it was the echo of Baba's van and screeching brakes that brought us all back to the reality. Ritchie rushed to open the gate for the two of them and before we knew it our blissful supper had been tossed into the midnight air. 'Oh! So, this is what you two get up to when we go out!'

Mama retorted, 'We have just been having a lovely evening, just the three of us.' See how I'm always included now, so I must truly be her son. 'Our evening has been spoiled. Bablu, we may as well go to our beds,' Mama said sadly.

'What! No supper for us!' said greedy Baba. 'No,' said Mama, 'supper is before 10 pm.' Mama quickly reached for my chicken before the big hairy spade of Baba's hand encroached upon it. 'Oh! I was hoping to finish that up.' Baba moaned. 'Bruno hasn't even started yet' replied Mama. 'Pass me Bruno's plate, Bablu, I will hand-feed him.'

I loved it when Mama fed me. It reminded me of when I was a little baby, although I'm not much bigger now, and I'm wiser. When Mama tells me to go for wee-wee, I can manage the steps by myself now and I totter under the little patch of grass that awaits me daily.

I love it when I go back up the steps myself. The marble seems to know my worries about slipping and it gently grips my baby feet so I'm safe. I haven't asked it to do this, it just did. I told you this house is magical! We silently walked through the sparkly courtyard with the bronze hanging lamps and the turquoise blue fountain in the middle of the courtyard with the sparkly mirrors on it, silently we would go for one nightly sleep. I too was asleep in Mama's arm, and Mama gently lifted me on the new embroidered bed cover. I had grown so much in the past few months so she made me a new one. She said good night to Bablu and pulled back the beautifully embroidered pale golden cover for her bed. She loved this cover, she bought it from Jodhpur and said as soon as she went into the shop she saw the cover placed immediately on the countertop as she opened the door of the shop, her eyes directly sailed to the beloved cover and Mama without any hesitation cradled it in her arms and asked the staff to pack it for her. Mama said that she could never have found anything as perfect anywhere in the whole wide world.

Everything in Mama's house was loved and she would cry if anything was accidently broken. The dishes had to be washed one by one and polished with the white linen towels from Ireland. Apparently Ireland was one of her ancestral homes of which she has many fond memories. One of her uncle's lived in a beautiful grey stone castle, near the sea, and often she would sit on one of the terraces and gaze into the distance. Into the clouds she could foresee her future. And one day she saw her beloved in the clouds riding gallantly on a white stallion. Some months later her prophecy was fulfilled, he discovered the Gallic castle and their eyes met in space, instantly they married with the love of their family and village.

But tragically, as quick as he came, he left into the clouds. One early morning on a ride with his beloved horse, he went riding in dense fog, and overlooked a sharp hanging cliff. The two stumbled and rode into the stormy, icy ocean. Mama's heart was broken into immeasurable pieces like the universe. Without talking to her loved ones, she packed her very little belongings and went to Dublin and caught an ocean liner to India where she sailed to Mumbai. She had only read about India and knew not one person there, all she knew what she felt was to be her destiny. Mama hired a companion who's family had multiple businesses in Mumbai. Together they travelled for six months by train around southern India until they entered in the state of Goa where it is said that once in many months did my Mama feel at peace. I know no more of this sad tale – perhaps Mama will tell more in the years to come.

Daily they travelled, Mama and her companion. She was a good companion to her and slowly-slowly she began to smile her smile. Her smile, it was said, was as warm as the Goan sky with its palm-fringed horizon. One lovely perfect day they had travelled for many hours until it was almost sunset when Mama saw in the nearby distance an old Goan mansion, dilapidated and unloved. It stood on an empty hill with nothing around it but mango trees and cotton-bud trees. Although it looked lonely it also had a look of happiness, for it knew in its heart that today it would have a companion for the rest of its life. They disembarked the 'silver cloud car' and walked towards the broken steps of the new abode. In fact, it was fourteen years ago that the house was abandoned but the energy as soon as Mama entered was enlightened from above and the feeling of the intense adoration from the universe cocooned it in love.

The roof was totally broken, some of the beams were hanging from the elevated ceilings. The plaster had been eaten by red ants and the beautiful shell window had been broken either with cricket balls or the high monsoon winds. Bats nested in the loft but left their hellos on all of the undressed walls. Cattle meandered in and out of the doorless mansion on broken steps, one lonely light bulb hung from the front entrance but of course there was no electricity. Electricity was not needed, for the heavens lit every nook and cranny of the ramshackle mansion. I loved it with all my heart. Mama's companion from Mumbai stood speechless as he listened to her 'I have never seen you so positive before, my dear Elizabeth, in the short time I have known you,' said Sudhir. 'My friend, this opportunity has not happened to me before. This is certainly a gift from the universe and I need a home. I am independent now and my future is here. Piara, I'm going to call her, and from tomorrow we begin celestial plans for repairing and redecorating my beloved Piara,' Elizabeth replied.

Sudir enquired, 'Why do you call her Piara?'

'Well, Sudhir, a long time ago I read a book called The Life of the Bhagat Puran Singh. He was from the Punjab where he lived and took care of the homeless, deformed and poor people that nobody wanted. Each day he would beg for alms to feed and shelter them all. He devoted his life to these unwanted beings. Way before Mother Teresa was on the scene. One day he was walking past the rubbish tip when he came across a child about eighteen months old that had been thrown upon the tip. He was crippled and was living off milk given by the locals from cows with dysentery. It was a pitiful site. Bhagat Puran Singh took pity on him and carried him home. He loved the boy so much he named him Piara, which means "the loved one" in Hindi and he referred to him as the "garland of flowers around my neck". So, Sudhir, Piara is my loved one and I'll take her from brokenness to beauty. She will be so beautiful that people will come from all around to feel her energy and be inspired by her greatness. From this day on she is my mission, just like the boy Bhagat Puran Singh adopted.'

It took almost two years for Piara to be born and my Mama told me she would often sit outside in her little Nano car and gaze at her from outside. The beautiful flamingo birds on the gate that Mama had created. She painted and adorned their eyes with emerald jewels. The beauty of Piara made her think of the divine and her connection with Him. There would be no Piara and I would not belong to the wonderland of the heaven if it were not for the Divine.

BABA'S SKULLDUGGERY

After breakfast the next morning Mama went to the beauty parlour. I was left alone with Bablu, Baba and Ralph. I tottered in and out of the house patiently waiting for Mama to return. She seemed to be gone for hours. Both Baba and Ralph were sitting on the balcony smoking their dog-ends and drinking their beer out of Mama's handmade brown goblets and Bablu was probably cleaning the pool at the back of the house.

I started to climb the steps of the veranda, and when I reached the top I was preparing to have a little drink of water from the copper dish that was adorned with white water lilies. I felt a jolt on the back of my collar. I was hoisted six feet in the air by a giant hairy arm, wearing countless Rakhi bracelets (where did he acquire all this Rakhi sisters)! I was tucked under an armpit and I admit I knew it was not Bablu's, because Bablu's armpit was fresh as the morning dew. I couldn't see because my eyes were placed in such a position that all I could see was Superman's belt, and an overwhelming stench of manure came from an armpit, but the Superman belt made me realise the culprit. He threw his gargantuan bottom onto the pale pink marble and threw me in the air. I thought I would be hanging in the silver light fitting for ever. Mama would never think of looking for me there, and my whimper would never be heard. I could be a part of the light fitting forever. Oh! I just realised I had an amazing jolt of realisation this would be only for few hours because at 6 pm Bablu would turn off all the lights and I would be noticed when Mama came to the veranda for the evening meal.

Seconds later, and unattached to silver light fittings, I found myself next to the Superman's belt and two huge hairy hands. My brain told me it was Baba that was the culprit my little teeth were chattering and my heart was fluttering. What an utterly stupid thing to do to this little beautiful child of a dog, namely me. I thought whatever love I had for him was now gone and I would watch for every shadow that came to me in the future.

'What a stupid thing to do, Baba,' said Ralph. 'In the state you are in you could easily missed catching him.'

'Never in this world,' snorted Baba. 'You know I am Baba; Baba's are magical and nothing ever happens to a Baba.'

Ralph gave him an astonished look and replied again. 'Here we go again, Baba, guru of the gurus. Your imagination goes beyond the realm of the reality. I give up with you here! Give Bruno to me, you stupid man, and don't touch him again.'

Oh, I didn't know Ralph could raise his voice, as he was always so quiet, but I suppose it was difficult for words to come out of his mouth because he always had to compete with Baba's mouth or he had a dog-end stuck to his lips which was connected to a draft of smoke or a brown goblet of Kingfisher which was on a journey to his mouth that was patiently waiting for parking space between its two cracked brown lips that was topped off with a what looked like a handmade moustache, that looked like it was made up of broomcorn which was used to make sweeping brushes. His teeth looked handmade as well, as they were almost horse-size but beautiful, apart from some brown lines of crayon or paints.

I don't know why he did that, they would look much better without them and he had a bright red tongue like tortoises, apparently from something called betelnut. But thankfully Ralph saved the day and I sat happily on his lap until Mama took charge. There was to be no mention of this occurrence while Mama was there, she would be so upset about it all. I don't like heights and the bright light would have hurt my beautiful brown eyes. Thankfully Ralph had some common sense and saved that day. I think I like his striped teeth now as I looked closer at them, but his moustache was so prickly that it hurt my little tongue when I gave him a kiss and slurp of gratitude.

I think Mama's golden bottle of hair juice would work on his moustache perfectly. But I didn't know how to ask Mama for a favour. I wish I did, and then Ralph's prickly moustache would be much cuddlier, if it is to ever happen again. I hope it never does because that was pretty heinous. I saw things from that height that I never want to see again. So many little creepy spiders and a dead lizard hanging precariously on the top hook of the light fitting with its long pink tongue hanging until it had completely dried, just like the Bombay ducks drying on the seashore.

Mama looked beautiful tonight with her sapphire blue gown and auburn locks flying in the evening breeze. Some heavenly mimosa sat behind her diamond clip on her hair. Bablu the guard wrapped his arm around her waist, guiding her to her seat. She was an exotic butterfly, delicate and pretty, with unknown and mysterious qualities about her. She mesmerised everyone around her and everyone would be waiting to hear her sweet voice: 'So there you are my son...'

Gently she lifted me from Ralph's lap, I keep looking at Mama to see if she noticed Ralph's moustache, which of course she did. But it's too polite to mention the condition and the state of his moustache, when all of a sudden it was as if Ralph was reading my mind. Ralph asked Mama a question: 'Elizabeth! I hope you don't mind, as I've been staying in Goa I've noticed that my moustache has become very hard and dry. I don't suppose you know of something which can make it softer?'

'Hmm, let me look, Ritchie. Let's see if some of my lovely conditioner will work wonders for it. I will give it to you later but I advise you to put it on tomorrow. Also if you do it tomorrow it won't stain in the bed covers tonight.'

Mama was being her usual lovely self, helping Ralph, when Baba butted in, 'Does no one want to do anything for me around here? Look I have a big hole in my satin trousers since I've been here and not one person has offered to repair it!'

'Oh, don't be such a jealous big baby, Baba – I'll ask Urmila to repair it. Do you have anything else to wear while this is going on because your trousers look more than worse for wear and need washing. You have been wearing the same pair ever since you came,' Mama said in a concerned manner.

'No, only my lungi,' he replied. The sight of Baba running around Piara and possibly the village was too much for Mama to bear thinking about.

'OK, after dinner I will ask Bablu to fetch some jeans from the market. What size are you Baba? Your waist size I mean?'

'I think I'm a size thirty,' said Baba in an unconcerned way.

Everyone started to roar with laughter, except Mama. She never let a raucous sound escape from her pretty pink lips. Not ever!

'What do you mean, and why are you laughing?' retorted Baba. 'I'm the same size as I was at school.' Again, another set of raucous laughter came even louder than the one before. Ralph held his chest and bravely tried to silence his laughter and he bet a packet of Woodbine on the fact that Baba had a size forty-two waist. Baba asked for the Woodbine now.

'Bablu, dear, would you purchase some blue jeans after serving our dinner. Size forty-two should be correct,' asked Mama.

Ralph quickly picked the Woodbine from Baba's spade-like hand and hid them in his shorts back pocket.

'That's what I don't like about you, Ralph, you never fulfil your bets.'

'Bet or no bet, Baba, you are at least forty-two-inch waist. I think you have to use your Superman's belt to bridge the gap.'

Baba was not too quick to catch on about the gap and so replied that he hoped Mama would pay for them to be taken in when he proves them to be too big!

'OK, that's enough, everyone, enough of this.' Mama tried to calm down the row. 'You won't even be paying for them as normal,' she said.

Bablu served up a delicious avocado salad with tomato and cucumber and sprinkled with delicately cut spring onions and covered with a lovely honey and mustard dressing. But Mama would only allow me to have the avocado. She said that tomato and onion were not good for little dogs. Next came a juicy bowl of soup sprinkled with mace. I was allowed quite a grownup menu but I really enjoyed the main course of roast chicken and roast potato. I loved it because Mama always fed me. It was my most precious part of the day and Mama always blew from her delicate lips twirls of heavenly puffs onto pieces of crispy roast potato.

'I really shouldn't do this, my darling Bruno, it isn't polite to blow on someone else's food, but you are my precious baby son, so I will make an exception,' Mama said adoringly.

I could see Baba was furious at the attention I was getting, his eyes bulged in his eye sockets and his face becoming red with anger. Mama asked him why he had to hang around her shoulder every time she fed the baby. 'Just checking his manners, Liz, that's all,' Baba answered curtly.

'I've told you before, Baba, don't call me Liz!! It's Elizabeth, as my Mama and Papa christened me.'

Baba grumbled under his breath while trying to compose some sort of a plan.

'That Bruno is giving me a hard time, Ritchie. She has no time for me now that he is on the scene, she hardly talks to me. All it is, is "Bruno this and Bruno that,"' Baba grumbled to his partner in crime.

Ritchie replied, 'What do you mean, Baba? What is peeving you? You are not normally like that!'

'You will soon find out, Ritchie, all in good time. That is all I'm going to say to you at the moment…' a perturbed Baba replied.

THE PLAN IS HATCHED

The next day Mama went out in her Nano. She would be out for several hours and told me to be careful while she was away. I gave Mama a doggy nod and a little sad look appeared out of my baby eyes. I felt that my eyes were dropping to the floor but no crocodile tears came. So I suppose I was becoming a grown-up baby boy who was sensible instead of moping. I don't know if I'm too happy about growing up, not so much cuddles and kisses. No more loving hugs but I was clearer in my head. The years bring another kind of love and responsibility. But that was for years to come, no need to worry about it now.

I was toddling around the compound of the mansion with my white chewy sticks in my mouth. I think that they are like the dummies that mummies and daddies give to their babies when they are bored and whining.

I trotted around the beautiful gardens looking for any newborn flowers or pretty coloured butterflies that would land on my head tickling my nose with their whiskers. They were nice to play with, but suddenly I was picked up by Baba's brutish hand and thrown up to his face. 'Oh, oh what is the little master doing all by himself, no one to watch him in all in this big-big place where no one can see him or see what is happening…'

This statement sounded a little frightening to my brain. Never mind,

Ritchie was there so I was relatively happy nothing would happen to me in the presence of Ralph, he had become a friend and he would walk around the garden with me throwing my chewy sticks for me to catch but I never could catch then. Mama said I was just like her, all butterfingers, which meant that our hands were full of butter and the ball would keep slipping through our hands. I've never seen her do it but I imagine its true. Mama would never tell a lie to anyone.

Baba caught the chewy stick while Ralph went inside the house for his cigarette but Baba picked me up and never uttered a word. He walked to the main flamingo gate onto the access path outside. Oh what do I do now? I'm a bit chubby to crawl through any hole. Then he threw the chewy stick on the road: 'Go on, go on, Bruno-Bruno. Just look at that lovely juicy chewy stick. Hurry up and get it before the street dogs get it,' ordered Baba. I started to trot after the rolling chewy stick when I heard Ralph's voice shouting at me. 'Bruno-Bruno, you must never go out of the gate. There are lots of horrible things can happen to you outside this big-big gate. This gate protects all of us, especially you, Bruno, because you are so tiny and helpless and we would all be very upset if anything happened to you.'

I didn't understand what 'if anything happened to you' meant but I knew it wasn't something nice, so my little body shook a little with fright and I left the stick for the poor little street dogs. Ralph opened the gate and lifted me in his arms and kissed the top of my head. 'Oh! Bruno, never do that again. Mama's heart would break and we never want this to happen to her.'

I snuggled into Ralph's chin as much as I could. I never wanted to see the sky again.

The sky was a pathway from uncertainty to safety for me. The sky in the courtyard was different, it looked bluer and the clouds were fluffier and friendlier. The courtyard sky was friendlier to me and I would only watch the courtyard sky until I felt safe again. When Ralph retold the tale to Baba, all he could say was, 'I told you so – that little bugger is more trouble than he's worth, quite frankly I can't see what Liz sees in him. I wish I never brought him now.'

Ralph shook his head, forgetting I was under his stubbly chin. I sustained many hairlines scratches to my cranium that lunchtime, but the pain soon went when I was handed over to Mama who smothered my little head in sweet-smelling kisses.

'Bruno, you must never go out of that gate again. Tomorrow we will put some plastic netting on the gate that will keep you safe from now on. You will never be able to squeeze through it again,' Mama said in a concerned voice. Oh, if only Mama and Ralph had known what had really happened. I really think Baba does not like me, or he is jealous of me, for why will he pass me through a big gate like that? I didn't think it was funny at all. In fact my little bottom was still hurting me, my luscious thick auburn coat became ironed to my skin. I didn't ever want to experience that again. My fur didn't look good at all!

The evening passed without any problems, and in the morning I woke up without disturbing Mama at all.

I sashayed with confidence through the inner courtyard and into the main courtyard then into the hall of the golden gate. Suddenly yesterday's episode came back into my mind. Baba was sat on the balcony entrance all by himself and had the look of mischief on his face. Hmm… I had a big problem in my hands now because he had just seen me – what should I do? Just take a chance and run out and pass him. Although I knew my legs were not as fast as his hand. I could be throttled by his gargantuan hand as fast as my little legs could reach the first step.

I decided to turn back towards Mama's room and trot a little as to give the game away. What game! I was really frightened yesterday, he tried to feed me to the local lions (namely the local dogs) and goodness knows what he had planned for me today before. I knew it, I would hide behind Bablu's blue plastic mop and bucket. I was really happy because I tricked him. But then I forgot about my baby tail that was thick and bushier with a prominent black stripe down the middle which was now pointing six inches to the north pole …Oh, no, he saw me…

'Oh, so you think you are hiding from me do you, my lord! Well, you've forgotten your Baba has got magical powers and I can do anything. I virtually can anything I want to do even without trying. Watch me jump, Bruno! Just watch and then find me. Close your eyes first, Bruno, and when I count to ten you can open your eyes.'

Luckily, I could count to ten. In fact I can count to twenty, but beyond that was not necessary. I would never challenge to those depth about anything. I reached ten in my little brain very quickly and opened my tightly shut eyes, for I would never cheat by keeping one open. I could do that, keep one that I need open to see, but I had given my word and so I would act accordingly. Slowly I opened my eyes and for some seconds I experienced overall blackness. I moved my head side to side and back and forth and could then see normally.

Now where was that Baba? I trotted around the courtyard and kitchen trying to imagine where he could be but Baba was nowhere to be seen, now what do I do? The locks to the dining room were securely tightened from the outside so he couldn't be in there. I imagined him being in one of the large courtyard cupboards where Mama kept her art materials but he was in neither.

Looking at the shallow depth of the shelves, I could understand why, but where was he! I toddled through the golden gate when I started to remember. A spade-like hand grabbed me from behind but there was no hand to be seen. I slowly crept down the veranda steps and was becoming increasingly nervous, when all of a sudden two bucket hands pulled me off the veranda steps.

'Ha-ha! I have got news for you!' growled Baba.

What news? I tremblingly thought, what's going to happen to me now? And where was Ralph and Bablu when I needed them. But most of all, Mama – where was she?

It's past her breakfast time. Something was very wrong and I was starting to get very worried – I needed my friends around me. I was the precious commodity in this village but I could never accept what would ever happen to me. Quickly Baba opened the door of his Maruti van and slung me to the floor. What had I done to deserve this treatment? I've only been nothing but nice to him, so many times I've purposely left succulent pieces of chicken on my plate, for in my reasoning they were his because his eyes had devoured them already time and time again and this act took away my appetite.

Anything his eyes had rolled over dozens of times my stomach told me to leave and allow the eyes that were bigger than his stomach to devour. I would make sure I ate every morsel in future. Sometimes kindness to a person is not appreciated, one has to learn from one's experience and move on.

But just where was I going to move on to and when? He screeched his brake while going through the huge outside gate with the beautiful flamingos on I was really getting worried. I rolled round and round the metal floor.

Some pieces of broken steel stuck in my little paw. If only the flamingos could talk, they would know where everyone had gone. But here I was in the Superman's super-dirty van and with no idea of what was going on or what was going to happen to me. I really was frightened so I thought I would talk to Mama's friend God. I asked him to look after me and deliver me back quickly to the safety of my home. I was becoming too cocky, I heard Baba say of me one day, 'He is roaming around this house as if it were his.' He said. 'He is far too cocky this little half breed.'

I cried so much but I understood what he meant and perhaps I must take his comment on board or I would never want my Mama say this about me. I would never hurt her intellect. I could never hurt anyone, except perhaps Baba.

My heart was very frightened of him, but here I was trapped in his dirty and dangerous van. At the speed of light he raced through the double gate. I tossed and turned until I found a plastic strap attached to the back door. I clung for my life as we whizzed through the village when suddenly we came to an apparent stop. I huddled under the back seat with my front legs firmly attached to the plastic straps. I was sure I was completely hidden when the sliding door shutter opened, letting in all the Goan sunshine. My little white paws gave the game away. 'There you are you little bugger. See all the trouble you have given me. Now I have to devise a plan so your stubby ugly face won't see the light of day again in Piara again. I'm fed up of you spoiling plans with me and my Liz.'

Ooh! If I could speak I'd show him who had a little stubby ugly face. The cheek of it! But I'm here all by myself for no one to rescue me. Baba got out of his torn denim pocket, his fifteen year old Nokia phone that surprisingly worked as good as the day it was given as a gift to him by a fisherman friend. The Nokia had been thrown down many times and buried under tons of sand which would blow into his veranda at night when he had stumbled home drunk from the Chinese eateries, and the Nokia would find its own bed for the night. Wherever Baba fell the Nokia fell. He dialled someone called Raju.

'Raju, are you in?' he said.

'Yes!' replied Raju, 'why?'

'I've got a little problem and I need your help and there will be a little something in it for you,' Baba promised.

Oh, no! A little something – does he mean me? Am I the little something? I'll never see my Mama or Bablu ever again. My surrogate mama and papa are but a distant memory and I am only six months old. What misery lies ahead of me. Just what have I done wrong? Just replaced himself by me in my Mama's heart. It is like that in life, sometimes in life you are in love with a sardine bone and the next time you have fallen for a juicy chicken breast. The law of the universe is beyond our control. Will I be another hungry unloved lion of the street, or would I simply die of a broken heart? I think the latter, to be true – without my Mama's smile each morning I would simply shrivel and die. And I know for certain that there is no vacancy on the street of Bastora because I was only told of this yesterday by the street lions. All territories are totally full, that is until the next fatality, either road accident or starvation.

How do these street lions survive on crusts of dry bread or scattered handfuls of rice from the labourers that work on the road? God only knows how they manage it because they have very little for themselves. I have seen so many times myself. Mother serves father and then up to seven or eight children, and what's left from the children's and husband's plate goes to her, and what she can spare goes to the street lions – the street dogs.

These migrants from all over India are the untold relatives of Mama's friend God. No one notices their empathy or love for these street dogs except another friend of God, mainly my Mama. One day she told me a story of giving a group of the road workers a huge pile of clothes from her grandchildren and many guest that stays at the house from time to time, their reaction to this quite ordinary gesture simply overwhelmed Mama. She told me that the next day she was sitting on the balcony with Bablu and they all came to the gate and shouted for Bablu. Bablu dutifully walked to the gate to allow them in.

They all walked through the big gate like soldiers. Every one of then in some piece of clothing, even if it was far too big for them. The line was headed by a young girl of ten, Mama thought because of her height and undeveloped body. Mama later found out that she was fourteen and married with a small boy child, who tugged her long dress incessantly until he managed a response from her, which was just a nod and he became quiet straight away. Although she was only young it was easy to see why she was chosen to be the spokesperson. She had the confidence of the head girl at school and the personality of a soul who knew exactly her worth in this three-world culture, simply because she was never a member of this third-class society, but a person in her own right. A rarity in this country called India, where class and cast was a number one ruling.

In her outstretched arm was an aluminium plate full of white water lilies and a packet of tiger biscuits placed in the centre. Without asking Mama's permission to speak, she spoke in clear and educated voice. 'Madam, we are all here today to thank you for your kindness of the European clothes. You sent your guard with them yesterday and we were all so happy and will remember for the years to come. As you can see, we are all wearing a piece today, and may I say that I was so happy when I found this pink dress covered in daises yesterday. I think I look almost an English madam. Madam, don't you think so?'

Mama smiled and told her that if it wasn't for her long lustrous black hair wrapped in a pink ghoonghat (an Indian head scarf) she could be the prettiest madam in the Bardez.

With that remark she made the glorious girl giggle.

Mama told me she took the gift of flowers and biscuits gratefully. Everyone clapped and the party moved back through the big gate, never to be seen again.

What happens if I never see Mama again! What happens if I never hear any of her magical stories, which were where all stories of love and gratitude to her friend God.

Soon the van stopped, and with a clash of the sliding door Baba's big hands dragged me out of the spiky black door. Luckily I didn't cut my little paw again and he picked me up in his big bulky arm. I was quite big now and even he had a struggle to lift me. My head was dangling six inches from the ground and I had to quickly remember to not let my tongue drop from my mouth. It was now covered with daisy leaves and sand and bird poo. I was really choking, and the big brute was sweeping the floor with my lovely pink tongue. All I can say is I hope my smelly baby bum was stuck right his bushy whiskers. I never have a smelly bum but he caught me in his big burly arms before I had finished my ablutions in a proper manner!

'You smelly little bugger, Bruno, when did you last have a bath?'

In my mind I wanted to say 'much later than you, my lord,' but unfortunately, he was not educated in doggy talk and would never be able to converse with any mammal in any way shape or form. So I could only think of my sarcastic reply.

It was quite dark now and there was only a baby moon at first. When I first saw the baby moon I thought it was local decoration in a nearby village, but I looked at it daily and was in awe of its sparkles. It would always sparkle on the little thingamajigs by the golden gate. And sometimes when no one was around we would skip around the veranda with the golden gate until we were too tired and would fall asleep on the spot. I'm so sorry to say when that happened it would accidently frighten them by dropping my chubby fat paw on their lovely glittery bodies. But mostly now they knew the programme of our child's play and would avoid close proximity to my chunky spiky paws. So we all knew our place and everyone was relatively safe.

Why is my mind getting carried away from this horror story? Here I am still under Baba's smelly armpit and not knowing what was happening. He placed me on a muddy path and tied a rope around my neck, he tugged on it until my little tongue came popping out of my mouth. 'I don't know what is happening,' I said to my tongue. We are in a lane, in a compound with two small houses on the end of the lane and now Baba is walking towards one of them.

'Raju,' shouted Baba. 'Raju, where are you, I need your help.' What help, I wondered, is it a doctor? I'm sure we don't need doctor's help, because when Mama sees my little paw she will do the necessary. 'Coming, my friend, coming!' Raju shouted.

Although he didn't live in this village, Baba had incredible power over everyone. Everyone thought he was super-human because of his gigantic size and that he would get engaged in his magic tricks that everyone, including Mama, Ralph and myself, could not understand. So all in all when he told everyone he was a Baba everyone believed him and was in awe of him, and mostly because of his features revealing what he had done in his life for the community and his family. When in fact the deeds for his family were descending upon them when they least accepted it and somehow sucked away cash from friends and relatives of such premier disasters and miracles which he had read in the newspapers.

When there were no logical answers for these phenomenon he would weave himself intrinsically into them and the awaiting audiences would wait patiently and in awe of the outcome of the tale, and all of them were so happy to have a Baba in their village in Gorai. It was said that he never paid any ferry fares and the local restaurants would open their arms for him in the hope of a full house.

Baba knew how to react to the audience, and after drinking many Jack Daniels and cokes he would be conversing with rings around the tables, from various businessman and the local panchayet to various policeman from that area, there was a circle of almost of hypnotism around that area at those moments.

But here I am now in Bastora, still stuck under the most infamous armpit from Gorai. My tongue was still inches from the floor and my little bottom was for all to witness back here in this little Bastora house.

'So, who have we here, Baba' Raju said. 'This is Liz's little itsy bitsy baby, Prince Bruno,' I heard Baba reply with a jealous tone, 'and I have plans for this little runt. He is nothing but trouble, so I told her to get him trained before he was six months old because after that it was virtually impossible.'

Raju quizzically asked, 'What do you mean by getting him trained, Baba, are you putting him in circus ?'

Baba replied firmly, 'Of course not, just obedience and command. I brought a trainer for her once to the house and he was not cheap, and on the second training visit she saw him kick Bruno with his big black boot.'

I had whimpered and went running for safety to Mama. 'What a brute, don't worry, Bruno, he won't come again. Training can be done with either kindness or with love, and I am never allowing the former. Phew! I was glad I saw that, you can go now!' said Mama, 'and here is your full course of money. I will train him if he needs it. I saw your big foot on his side.' The trainer answered with audacity: 'I can assure you, madam, the boot would not cause any permanent damage. I can use my laser instead.'

'Please get out of here now!' Mama had said in a matter-of-fact manner. 'I never want to see your boots again and here is your full money so you don't bad-mouth me wherever you go.'

It's like that here, people are quick to bad-mouth you and then they profess that they are big churchgoers at the same time. Raju took me from Baba's armpit which was quite a difficult process. 'Nice looking dog, Baba! What breed is he?' asked Raju.

Baba replied, 'No idea about the breed but I'm sure there is hound in him. Look at his ears, and look at his paws. They are not ordinary paws, they are big paws and have big claws. This dog is some type of hound...'

'What are you going to do with him?' asked Raju.

'Well firstly I'm going to make his mama really cry by pretending he is lost. When all the time he will be locked in your kitchen. We can make some money from him, the little runt, I'll teach her to love him instead of me – after all, I met her first. She is my property and after she is gone all this house and land will be mine.'

When is she gone? Gone where? My little heart started to shake. Is she leaving me already. Oh, I could hardly think of such a thing – we had only just found one another and I loved her with an unbelieve love I couldn't explain. I was thrown under a greasy dining table with nothing on it. I could tell this was a poor house – a table with no cloth! A settee made of aluminium with a velvet Goan cover that clashed with everything it came across, as my Mama in Gorai will call it: 'VILE.' My Mama in Bastora wouldn't say anything but just close her eyes, but of course none of my friends could even envisage my dreadful ordeal in this empty Goan house.

Baba produced some rope from around his waist and wrapped it double around my shaking neck and the other end tied around the table leg. 'From here on, you little mutt, this is your life!'

Raju put some water in a steel vessel in front of my delicate nose. I think I'll die of water deprivation before long. Where was my glass bowl

with sparkling spring water? Where was my lovely chicken!? Why are they doing this to me? I have never done anything wrong to him except giving Baba a dirty look when he told someone I was a spoiled brat, but I'm not and I have Mama to confirm the fact. According to her I'm adorable and beautiful and understand every command given to me. I was a true academic, although I truly didn't know what the word academic meant. All I had pertained from the sentence was that I was above normal intelligence and with an abundance of common sense.

The rope tightened until it became only fourteen inches long, I couldn't even turn my body around in the length that was left, all I could do was to lie on the filthy floor that was patterned with big foot marks, big boot marks and flipflop shapes of every size sprinkled with feathers and bodies of shrimps.

I had never seen anything like this mess before, even in Baba's house, and at least his floor was clean, even if it was only clean with maggot fat. I looked all around, there was nowhere to go, only to lie on the filthy floor and worry about what would happen next.

I could hear them whispering in the kitchen. What are they going to do with me now? My brain was doing somersaults and I was so nervous. I wanted to poo, at least the thought of keeping that at bay was keeping my thought away from the bigger problem. Perhaps he is only coming for a quick chat with his friend Raju but why tie me up? I've got impeccable manners. My Mama in Gorai always remarked upon how I piled my mackerel bones in a horizontal manner, and so neat and clean not even one crumb of flesh to be seen. And to keep my bowl clean I would double lick my little plastic plate.

Of course, at Mama's house in Bastora I never had to do anything. Bablu did everything for me, so this abode was a far cry from anywhere I had been in my short six-month life. There were no lights in this broken house only the moon shining through the roof and two candles placed in the kitchen. I was a little bit nervous. I don't like darkness, you couldn't see anything even close by. They were talking quietly and then I heard Baba say, 'Matter of fact, I'll do what I told you, you do what I said to you, it's at as easy as pie and if his master makes any sound, you just pull the rope around his neck tighter – he'll soon get the message…'

I was shivering with fear, I hoped my teeth would not start chattering because they will make noise and I will get the rope pulled tighter around my neck. I must be as quiet as possible or my fate will be hastened and I don't know what I have done wrong or why I'm here. Is my Mama

ME Having been captured
and Remembering Ma- Ma!!

unhappy with me? Have I been naughty? Without knowing I laid my head on the dirty floor and tried to sleep but his words kept echoing in my brain, 'Do what I told you to do! And don't do anything else until I contact you again.' Just what did these words mean? I can't think that I did anything wrong! I was just tottering around that garden giving a few ants and a dragonfly a little ride when suddenly I was lifted upside down by this spade-like human hand and thrust in the van. I was helpless. Where was Mama, or Bablu or Ralph when I needed them?

Meanwhile, I heard Baba's Nokia ring. It was Mama. 'Oh, thank God for that,' I heard him say. 'I don't know where he is, Liz, he's your dog, not mine.'

Mama was sad, saying I was lost and no one knew where I was.

But I was here! I wanted to shout, but where was here? Bablu was sent to look for me in the nearby facilities but came back empty-handed. I heard Mama and Bablu went out in the little Nano. Mama,, I believe was a bit hysterical, she was driving the Nano in a wild manner while shouting out from the driver's window, 'BRUNO, BRUNO, where are you, my son?'

Bablu tried his best to calm her down. 'There he is, Bablu there in the paddy field, see he is looking at us.' They stepped out and Bablu ventured in the paddy field while Mama continued to cry, 'BRUNO BRUNO.' This was all conveyed to me later on that evening. The dog was not me, obviously. Perhaps they were going to paint his black stripe on his back and swap him for me. Oh no! My brain is becoming too hyper. Surely no one can be so evil. Mama and Bablu drove on to the little grocery shop in the village. Mama's eyes were all swollen with crying and she was looking like a limp rag, I believe, when I was told this by Rex, Tereza's watchdog later that evening.

'Tereza! Bruno is missing! We searched all over the estate and even all around the village, just how did he get out of the compound?' Mama cried. 'I'm afraid he has been kidnapped,' said Tereza.

Oh! My joy, my happiness! The truth!

Mama fainted onto the countertop in the shop and Bablu caught her into his arms before she fell to the floor. 'Quick, Tereza, some water for madam and some smelling salts,' asked Bablu frantically.

'I have no smelling salts but this bottle of mosquito spray, Bablu, but make sure you don't spray it to close,' Tereza said helpfully.

Bablu quietly tossed the thought of the mosquito spray through his head and made the instant decision that it would help if it wasn't sprayed too close to her face.

Mama jostled with either the wetness of the spray or its deathly smell. Bablu lifted her into his arms and pulled the golden locks away from her ashen face, it was seconds before she spoke. 'Ooh, Bablu, what are we going to do my baby has been kidnapped. What am I to do?'

Tereza jumped to attention. Mama said she was salt of the earth – I don't quite understand what that meant but I think that was a nice comment because Mama was often walking to see her at her little shop down the road, and she only did that with one other person in the village and that was with Didi aunty who had a little brick and coconut leaf shack off-site by Mama's mansion.

Mama said that she felt sorry for Didi aunty because she was so thin, thinner than a blade of grass Mama would say with concern. Didi aunty was so downtrodden by life but she always managed a smile for Mama, but her little shop was God sent for her, almost a beautiful gold and a ruby crown. With this little shop selling only biscuits and rice it gave her enough money to feed her family of three.

Mama bought her a little fridge for Rs7000 with which she was overjoyed and now she could sell soft drinks as well as water. Mama was always buying her vitamin tablets and instructing her how to take them. Mama helped her as much as needed when she noticed a change in her appearance. Mama said she always wanted to cuddle her because she looked like she needed it. Mama said her beautiful black eyes would double in size, either with tears or emotions when Mama did this and even though she was so thin her short black hair was as shiny as the crow's blue-black feathers in the early morning sun. Apparently Didi aunty was another salt of the earth – perhaps there was a sisterhood in the village?

'I've got a good idea, madam!' said Tereza. 'Let's put a notice up in the shop about Bruno being missing and offer a reward.'

Bablu shook his head. 'I don't think so, madam, it would be a regular occurrence if we do.'

'I don't care,' said Mama, 'my baby is worth more than everything, more then everything I've got.'

Tereza produced a large card and black felt-tip pen, left a line empty, and in the middle of the line put the words 'REWARD TWO THOUSAND RUPEES for the return of Bruno.' Next line: 'Piara mansion,' and below that, 'Please ring Tereza on 8425671777.' 'It's best I put my number, madam, and not yours, can't be too careful.'

'You are right, Tereza, good thinking! My mind is still too upset to think straight,' Mama said, still shaken with grief.

Bablu drove the little white Nano back to the house and took Mama to her room, switched on her air-conditioner and swiftly bought her a nice strong coffee to calm her down. 'Try not to worry, madam, I've got a good feeling about this; Bruno will never venture beyond the gate, he is not a wondering dog. He is happy here with us at the house. I rather suspect some foul play, and seeing that Ralph is still in the house there is only one person missing…'

Mama perfectly understood Bablu's remark and looked perplexed at the enormity of the fact that within our small group of friends that there could be an enemy in our midst. 'You try to relax, madam, play some soothing music or do some meditation.'

Mama knew that this would not be possible so took her coffee to the pool and sat by the Champa tree in the water, with its enchanting musky perfume. A fresh petal landed on the floor where she was sitting. She remembered the beauty that had floated to her in the pool several weeks ago. She gently lifted it to her face to smell the perfume and kissed the exquisite petal, she held it away from her to take in all its beauty to her swollen eyes. 'You must have witnessed all this, my pretty Champa, if only you can tell me where my baby is. My heart is breaking with the thought of it,' Mama whispered.

The Champa tree wondered if she should reveal the garden secret. This was a magical garden belonging to the magical house. If she revealed the answer the magic would be gone, but she remembered the power of telepathy and sent such warm waves of love to Mama's hands who instinctively knew that everything would be OK.

Bablu had gone out again in the little Nano. Which direction would he travel in? He was trying to place himself in my position. But how could Bablu establish my whereabouts by simply thinking? This problem was beyond the normal, all he could do was hope. Bablu's phone rang in his pocket. His heart jumped because his little Nokia was hardly ever used, once a week he would ring his widowed mother in Kolkata – he seems to be a loving son!

'Hello, Bablu! I've just had a phone call from some unknown number. Hello, this is Tereza, by the way,' the caller said. She thought she had heard Bablu's heart jump at the thought of Bruno's return to home and to tell the news to Mama. When Bablu reached Mama's room, she laid prostrate on her golden bed, her arms were outstretched and in her left hand a perfect Champa flower. 'Madam, are you all right?'

Mama refused to recognise Bablu's voice; his voice and tears were still too busy clouding her beautiful blue eyes.

'We think we have found your son!' The swift turn of her body and she bolted upright and looked straight into his eyes, 'Where? Who's got him, Bablu?'

Bablu replied, 'I don't know, madam, but Tereza had just rang to tell me that someone called Raju thinks it is Bruno and he had him in his house. It's only around the corner. So I'll go now and check it out...'

Mama squealed with joy, but on those words shouted, 'Baba, Oh, Baba, we think we have found Bruno!'

'Oh, I didn't know that he was missing!' Baba replied unemotionally. 'I tell you that dog is nothing but trouble, just look at the state of you, you're like a person possessed. Where is he? I'll go and I'll get him...'

'Oh, I was going, sir, to bring him home – he may be frightened,' Bablu said, his voice full of warmth.

'Oh no! What are the pair of you doing – you are making him into a sissy. If you had trained him like I said this would never have happened. He would be a proper guard dog, which was what I intended in the first place. Never mind all these lovey-dovey things, a dog is a dog and he should work for his food and not be pampered like a baby, a little kick at the backside from the trainer is a good thing – it teaches them that we never accept disobedience.'

'Bruno, is my baby, not yours! You gave him to me as a gift,' Mama said with tears in her eyes.

'Yes! But I didn't know that he was to be as valuable as he is!' sniggered Baba.

'What? Valuable to you? Or valuable to me?'

Baba stood silent. Mama stood as tall as she could in defiance of him.

'You big brute, you are jealous of my son. As soon as you came here. You know I dislike jealous people, it causes negative energy in the house, and just see what has happened now. I do not trust you at all you brute!'

'Enough of this,' said Ralph. 'Let's go and see if it's Bruno or not. I'll come with you, Baba.'

'I'm coming also,' Bablu said, he wanted to say much more but his status in the house wouldn't allow it.

All three piled into the Nano and drove only five minutes. Baba seemed to know exactly the destination of the adored magi, Bruno. Ralph quickly exited the Nano, followed by Bablu out of the back door. 'I know this area well,' said Bablu, 'this is where the paddy workers lived.'

Baba knocked on the paint-free door in the matter-of-fact manner, not in a desperate manner (which is how it should be when searching for a beloved son). Ralph was puzzled. 'Do you know the people, Baba?' questioned Ralph.

'No, I've never seen or heard of them, why do you ask?' Baba guiltily retorted.

'Well, you didn't knock on the door like in a heist, it was as if you knew them!'

Baba continued, 'Well, I don't, I'm only here because of that blasted dog.'

The door opened at a suspicious pace. 'Hello?' shouted the voice, 'who is it?'

'It's Baba, from the advert!'

'Oh, you Baba? I was expecting Tereza…'

'No, I told her I'd come – a woman shouldn't venture out in the dark.'

Baba was really making it up as he went along.

'Hang on,' Bablu retorted, 'you weren't with us at Tereza's shop and when you were in the house you told madam that you had no idea that Bruno was missing.'

Bablu was smart and was highly suspicious of Baba.

'Shut your Bengali mouth, you servant, and keep it shut until I say so,' Baba chided.

With that, Bablu decided to whack Baba on his face, and fiercely defended himself: 'I'm standing no more abuse from you, you are no better than I am. I have plenty of land in Bengal, more then you have ever seen.' And with that Bablu landed one more almighty blow to Baba's face and he went flying to the filthy floor.

I knew Bablu's voice and began to howl. I had only howled once before when I knew I was in danger when Baba pushed me through the flamingo gate. That's what gave Baba the clue to my grandeur. When I howled out one almighty howl it spoke immediately of my hound bloodline in India – the hounds were a rarer breed then the mix of street dogs. I am a Kombai Hound, I have come to know, a Rajapalayam breed of the Malloraghita Kings but I had now given us a clue to my ancestors.

Bablu asked the houseowner his name. 'I'm called Raju,' he said. 'And how did you come across Bruno?' asked Bablu. 'Oh, I found him on the corner wall just sitting and looking.'

That was actually a habit of mine – I often sat on the steps of the wall in Mama's garden as it gave me height to survey the different parts of the garden. And often when I was sitting there I seemed to look as if I was going into a trance or deep meditation. Mama's friend Ina from Germany once said that I was her Zen master in another life.

Ina was a gentle soul and had an air of spirituality about her. She was a shaman by profession and would visit Mama once a year before the monsoon would start in April. Both Mama and Ina were best of friends – perhaps Ina and Mama were part of the sisterhood, but Mama said that Ina was the sweetest soul she had ever known and would love it if Ina came to live with her for ever.

'So, what do we do now?' asked Raju. 'I need to talk outside, Baba, about what you said earlier.'

Baba pulled Raju by the arm and splattered his huge hand over Raju's mouth. 'Watch what you say, my friend, or you'll experience my wrath.'

Once outside Raju asked for his two thousand rupees from Tereza. 'I saw Tereza's handwritten message on her reward noticeboard, but now we know you planned all this the reward is not available now,' said Raju

'Why you big bugger! What a liar you are!' said Raju. 'You came to my house this afternoon and told me to capture Bruno and in return I would get a two thousand rupee reward.'

By this point Baba is furious that his plan is not working. 'Well you are not getting anything now, you good for nothing rag picker.'

Raju was insulted. 'You know I'm a paddy boy not a rag picker, and the land is mine.'

Once again Baba tried to belittle Raju. 'What, 800 square metres? You call that land?' roared Baba, his laughter anchoring the broken roof on its way to the universe to be recorded into Bablu's twin soul. Mama explained all this to me one day when Baba shouted unkindly to Bablu when Bablu painted the gate with emulsion paint instead of gloss, but Mama liked it so much that she told him so, but Baba was jealous and called him some unkind words. Mama took offence to this – Mama was frightened of no one and would defend the lesser on any occasion.

Raju shouted to Baba, 'OK then, you lying cheat, I'll get you back in some other way – just be on your guard.'

Raju lifted his leg and hooked it over the broken seat of his ancient red, rusty, push bike with its two new tyres that he was hoping to pay for tomorrow with his reward money from that little scenario.

I stopped howling when I saw Bablu and Ritchie enter the room.

Ralph was very thin and it was so difficult to pick me up, so without asking Bablu happily obliged. Bablu was of such a kind nature, he never overstepped his mark, himself thinking Ralph was of a higher class.

With the safety of Bablu's armpit I was settled with haste, my tail waving in the air like a flag of victory.

Bablu, with the skill of a marionette, twisted me up in the correct way until I was in full licking distance of his smelly face. I fiercely licked my appreciation and Bablu flew with me down the road to Piara and to Mama, who was sitting with kind Tereza and both were relaying their stories to each other. Mama's face had returned to her normal pink but as

I was handed over to Mama's awaiting arms the tears came flowing again when she held me to her face.

'Well, Bablu! Tell me what has happened to my son before I go mad!' Mama begged.

'Well apparently, madam, Baba had seen on the computer the value of Bruno and his lineage. Although we knew of Bruno's history, we both knew that he was not a normal dog but someone of importance, and it seems Baba was going to capture him and leave him with a local called

Raju until he could find a customer for him, apparently. He is a Kombai hound, and he is needed for breeding purposes. His breed dated back to 500 BCE and was kept by the Marwa kings of Rajasthan to hunt bears, but our little notice in Tereza's shop spoilt everything for his plan. Raju saw the notice and rang Tereza who told Baba about the finding of Bruno, who immediately took us all to Raju's house. The plan has been spoilt – Baba spoke to Raju in the back room but he forgot that I speak Konkani fluently and I could hear every word of his wicked plan. So I grabbed Bruno and ran with him back to you, madam. I left Ralph in the kitchen and I ran with Bruno under my arms. Bruno was so excited he kept whimpering and licking my face but what's happening now I don't know. You've got Bruno back and that is what all matters.'

After much cuddling and hugging and terms of indulgence, Mama asked about Baba: 'I dare said he'll come back when he has concocted a suitable excuse.' With that remark came a shout at the entrance that called for Mama. Bablu went to see what it was. 'Madam, its Raju, from the paddy workers,' Bablu reported,

'Bring him through and ask him to sit down in the party room. I will see to him in due course.'

Tereza stood to leave, 'I better be going, madam, it's best I don't witness this, if only for my own sake. This village has more snakes in it then we can see!'

'OK, thanks, Tereza, for all your help! I'll pop and see you tomorrow with Bruno and Bablu when we go for a walk.'

Ralph came in shortly after with Baba. 'Madam would like to see you, Ralph,' said Bablu. 'She is in her room she asks me to send you in by yourself.'

This irked Baba. 'Something strange is happening here,' said Baba, annoyed that he was excluded from the scenario that was going to be re-enacted shortly.

Mama was very upset and she needed to find out the correct facts before making up her mind about the next step she would take. Meanwhile I was lying next to Mama. My face and feet were freshly wiped with fine white linen cloth soaked in rose water. The thought that her son had to lie on the filthy insect-laden greasy floor appalled her. Mama told Bablu they would give me a bath in the morning as it's too late now to do anything and I have been through such an ordeal and she didn't want me to be upset anymore. The rose-water freshener would calm me down and help me sleep after what could only be described as a horrifying ordeal.

Baba was well known for his fairy-tale excuses.

Ralph looked bemused when he entered Mama's room. 'Just what is wrong my beloved one?' he gently asked. 'You are looking so pale and shaken up, what on earth is wrong?'

Mama, remaining calm, answered, 'Well, nothing is wrong now, Ralph, but something dreadful happened today. My beloved son had been captured by some brute from the village. At first, I thought that Bruno was wandering around the garden checking on his little friends as he normally does,' said Mama, 'but I couldn't find him anywhere and neither could Bablu. We looked around Bastora, time and time again, and even as far as the highway, but couldn't find him. I was petrified with fear. I didn't know what to do next so I called at Tereza and she suggested putting up a notice of reward for him on the wall of her shop. Plenty of people would see the notice and when there was a reward of money the word would quickly go around the village, and if anyone had taken him the reward would quickly bring him back.'

'Is he here now?' said Ralph. 'Just how did you get him back?'

Mama explained: 'Well, Tereza had a phone call from a villager who said he had found him and took him back with him to try to find his owner. Raju said he tied him to the kitchen table and gave him some water, which he would not touch, so then he tried giving him some rice and fish gravy but again he would not touch it.'

Mama thought to herself that it was no wonder Bruno wouldn't touch the rice and fish gravy because even if she herself was starving she wouldn't touch the food, either – Bruno was not used to these leftovers. Bruno's food was specifically made for him and him alone. Raju was worried of him crying. 'Bruno was certainly disturbed,' said Mama, 'it was then that Raju heard a bang on the front door and it was the three of you.' Baba shouted, "Right, Raju, where is he! He's caused enough trouble today and now he needs to go home!"

'Exactly which home, Bruno thought – was it to be his first home to Gorai or was it to be with his Mama at Bastora who loved him beyond life itself?

'Raju shouted to Baba he is "not going anywhere until my two thousand is right here in the palm of my hand."

'Baba shouted, "You are having nothing now, you nincompoop, you are senseless! You rang Tereza to tell her of his recovery – what an idiot! How could I milk her for the ransom now? I was planning on a bigger ransom than a mere two thousand rupees."'

What a tale! Ralph listened intently with the few troubled wrinkles appearing below his peak of his Ralph Lauren hat. Ralph replied, 'I know nothing of this, all I did was follow the Lord's instruction and come with him, where and what to do he had no idea of, he just had to follow the instruction of the Lord as he always did.'

Although Ralph was instinctively universes way above Baba, he always treated him as the master and followed his every instruction or order; he always seemed in awe of Baba and would never answer him back and only followed his instruction, but this was about to change after a relationship of thirty years.

'Bablu, please bring Raju here,' said Mama, 'but don't allow Baba in, I want to hear Raju's tale first.'

Bablu turned immediately to fetch Raju, who by now was shaking and visibly tense, sitting on the big red leather chair in the corner – the size was rather gigantic but it looked from a distance that the chair was already giving him his punishment for a crime that was hardly of his doing. His eyes were popping out of his head and a salty sweat was running down his face, and he stumbled to his feet and zig-zagged across the floor. He didn't know what his punishment would be. Madam would be lenient with him although he didn't know of her as such, but he knew she had a good reputation among the locals and she was noted as quite a personality that would help anyone in distress, but harsh on anyone who deliberately troubled her. He hoped that she had not placed him in the latter category for he truly meant no harm to anyone, let alone her adored dog.

He stood upright with his hand behind his back, the sweat was dripping into his eyes making it look as if he was crying.

'Oh, sorry, what did you say your name was?' said Mama.

'I'm Raju, from around the corner; one of the paddy reapers.'

Ralph was sitting on a red patchwork settee and was waiting intently on the outcoming story on the stage. There was no cigarette in his hand tonight; he respected Mama's wish of no smoking in the house but his hands were shaking for his follow-up Old Monk rum, but he would have to wait for that.

Raju resided to madam with reverence. He had never seen her close up before and quite frankly was ashamed about the reason of why he was here to answer the question of this vision – that's just what she was, he thought, a vision! And a vision who loved this mutt of a dog. That was what Baba called him – a little dog who could be by her side and someone she could care for because he had heard that she had lost her husband some years ago and really didn't bother with acquaintances unless they were people with certain qualities, and these people were few and far between.

'Hello, Raju. I'm Elizabeth and I'm Bruno's mother.'

Raju at that point didn't know if he should laugh. But as he read her face he realised he should just stand still and listen. 'So, Raju, I would like to hear your side of this appalling story.'

Raju shuffled his square shoeless feet from side to side trying to get comfortable. Bablu handed him some tissues to wipe his head with – they were tissues of Christmas, red tissues with golden writing on and golden glitter shaken over them by madam.

Bruno was sitting by her side and from time to time madam would hold Bruno's hand and sprinkle golden glitter from the tissue. For some unknown reason Bruno loved all this sparkly thingamajigs, and it was so amusing to her but she was unaware that Bruno was first given to her on the veranda on that horrible monsoon morning when she lifted him from the red bag and gave him a cuddle and then placed him onto the veranda floor where myriads of the golden things were attached to the golden gate and hundreds had made their home on the veranda floor and benches. Those little thingamajigs held a special part in his heart, it was his second memory that was placed in his head – the first was, of course, his new Mama.

'Well, madam, l was just coming from the paddy field when I was stopped by Baba who asked me where I lived and I said just behind the black rubbish bin. "OK! That will do," retorted Baba, "show me the way. I need you to help me out just for a very short time, let's go to your house and I'll explain," Raju said.

'Baba said this dog was needed in Delhi so I was just going to keep him safe for a few days until the time to leave from Goa came about. It would be only matter of days and he would pay me for the duties performed – a sum of two thousand rupees which was four times my paddy field wages. I took the dog into the kitchen and he was crying I tried to calm him but he wouldn't let me touch him. So I tied him to the kitchen table when he started to howl. I've never heard anything like it, it frightened the life out of me. So, I left him alone, there was some leftover rice but he wouldn't touch it. He made me nervous so I just left him alone. That's when I heard a knock on the door and when I answered I heard Baba shouting and ranting, which disturbed me more. He called me rag picker, at which I was deeply affected, then from the other door two more people came in, neither of them speaking. One tall man who I presume was the security guard, who untied the dog and who obviously knew him because he didn't make a sound except whimpering and left with the guard.

'Baba came back into the room and noticed the dog and Bablu had disappeared, leaving only Ralph who perched himself on a red plastic stool. "Where is the dog Ralph?" he angrily shouted.

'"My God, you both are as useful as a chocolate fire guard, I ask you for help for one little thing and you mess that up, you are both gormless," he said.

'After that, he and Ralph ran from the house and I shouted, '"What about my money?" To which Baba replied, "You've messed that up now, you idiot, there is no reward for you."

'I said, what about my bike tyres, I owe Joseph money for the tyres? Angrily Baba replied, "That's your bloody problem, you don't expect me to pay you for nothing do you? You rag picking idiot!"

'With that I ran after Baba again to attack him with the rope that had been around Bruno's neck that had a large piece of lead pipe hanging from its end. It would certainly do damage to whoever was on the receiving end of this piece of equipment. Finally, I shouted, I'll get my revenge, think I'm stupid, do you? Let's just wait and see who is stupid I think you will be surprised!'

BABA GETS SUMMONED

'Oh, so that's what happened to my little son. He must have been terrified, poor thing. What a monster Baba is. Where is he now, Bablu?'

'He has gone back to the kitchen, madam, shall I bring him to you ?' Bablu replied.

'Yes please, Bablu, and take Raju back to the dining room and give him some water. I'll see him again in a few minutes '

Almost instantly, it was as if a huge bad energy had entered the room, the atmosphere had changed and there was a deathly silence. Baba entered the room and stood before Mama. So he could read her face he bowed until his jet black curls swept the marble floors.

'So, what is this summons for?' Baba retorted in a mocking voice to Mama.

In a voice, I have never heard before, Mama replied, 'Don't take that attitude with me, Baba, this is a very serious matter. I want you to tell me what has happened to my son.'

'I don't know why you are making such a fuss,' said Baba. 'Bruno only went for a play around.' While all this was going on Bruno was trying to hide in one of the sleeves of madam's kimono. His face safely secure so that he could witness nothing of this appearance of Baba. His feelings for Baba had clearly changed. He tried to shuffle up a little more but he couldn't move any further unless he pulled Mama from her sitting position.

Mama questioned Baba once more. 'I have been told by Raju that all this was your plan and that you had a wealthy buyer in Delhi for Bruno. Is this true?'

Baba thought quickly. 'Anything that has happened, has happened without me – I always get blamed for everything. It was the same at home. It was always me that got blamed for everything! That's why I left home at seven years old and went to live with grandpapa in Gorai.'

That journey benefited Baba because he became the apple of Grandpapa's eyes. Baba was a little con man from a very young age, so much in fact that Grandpapa left all of his land to Baba, ignoring all other members of the family. He said he left all his land purchases to Baba because he was the only one of his family that had any common sense.

Mama thought for a while, and then challenged the mystical Baba, 'So, if Bruno had only gone for a walk why was it until nightfall you started looking for Bruno. You know Bruno doesn't like the darkness unless he is with me and Raju tells me you had a buyer for him in Delhi.'

Baba was certainly perplexed. 'So, you'd rather believe a rag picker than me, your friend of six years? I am most offended by that and I don't think I'll be staying here for much longer. It's obvious that my friendship means nothing to you!'

And with that he marched out of the room with a rush of a hurricane and his black curly hair waving in an electric rage. Suddenly he turned around, and with a ranting red face roared: 'That's the last you ever hear from me, and let's see if that little runt of a dog Bruno can ever do as much for you as I have done.'

'Well, what can I say to that?' said Mama, and a look of bewilderment came over her face. 'All I know,' she said, 'is that this will never ever happen again. Bruno will never leave my side again!'

With that I was pulled from the middle of her sleeve and gently she placed me over her shoulder, her perfume of lilies made my heart feel so happy and my tears flew onto her silken skin. I was home for good and I would never leave my Mama's shadow. I would be the air that she breathed and the happiness that adorned her very presence.

When the theatre finished, Mama asked to see Raju once again. In the hallway Raju was less worried, but I wasn't, so I cuddled further into Mama's neck while I listened to the conversation. 'Raju, I realise that you are as much a victim of this stage play as Ritchie, but I'm more upset by Baba's action. I feel humiliated and stabbed in the back, his action is beyond normal reasoning.' Mama wiped her sparkly tears that fell on the dining cloth.

I tried to lick it up but it drained to quickly on the linen cloth, so I was disappointed about that. I've always wanted to own one of her tears so she would always be with me. I would never allow it to slip down my throat. I would rescue it and coat my little knuckles with it and it would be with me for ever and ever, and every time I felt sad I would think of its sparkle.

So now I know part of the story I will have to try to put it out of my mind.

'The main thing is that I have my son back with me and that should be the only thing that I have to worry about. I don't know what it is, I should be deliriously happy but I have an overwhelming feeling of doom, as if something really bad is going to happen.'

As soon as she said these words Bablu and Ralph ran to her side. Ralph threw his arms around her and pulled her close. I slipped from her shoulder and fell onto her bed.

Bablu, not knowing how to react to her, just stood and witnessed the scene. I think he longed to put his arms around her and kiss her tears away but he knew his position would not allow it to be.

In his heart he would do anything for her, for she was in his mind and soul. Mama knew it herself, but neither of them could find the courage to utter any words of love. But Ralph witnessed every moment and he himself was ashamedly shocked by himself for being consumed with this jealousy.

He was fifty-four years old and never had any feelings for any women. In fact, he was thinking he could never recollect ever having any conversation with any women except his mother and sisters, but here he was consumed unknowingly with feelings of some sort of concern for his friend Elizabeth.

'I don't know how to help with this, Liz,' said Ralph. 'Perhaps I should leave with Baba and then you can relax and enjoy your life with Bruno.'

Ralph dare not mention the fact that Bablu is deeply in love with Mama; for one he wasn't sure if his mind was playing games with him, and secondly, he didn't want to make the pathway free for Bablu. Now he was being childlike, he thought, but just what could he do – for once in his life he was not in control of his brain and this was the first time it had ever happened to him. Ralph wanted to speak of his love but he himself was unsure of his feelings. Things will be better tomorrow, he thought.

'Liz, why don't I make you a nice nighttime drink? Things will be better in the morning.' And with that my Mama said, 'I think it's time for bed, Bruno! Come here, my darling, and let Mama give you your night time kiss.'

I was placed by her bed in my new furry bed. I had outgrown my first silken bed but I loved this one much more because it was squashy and cuddly and made me think of my first night with my Gorai Mama and Papa, when we all cuddled together after eating the sparkly white wafers from the little white church. At this very moment I missed my old Mama and Papa so much my little heart started to flutter with love for them.

Without them I would never know of this life with Mama and probably be just another beach bum, begging and scratching for a pittance of existence instead of living in this wonderful house that was filled with love and happiness. That is until Baba constructed his dreadful plan. But now, I was going to my precious bed next to Mama's and tomorrow would be another day.

The next day did come, and I heard Mama stir from her bed so I decided to do the same but forgot I was in my new furry fluffy bed. I found it very difficult to manoeuvre, and it took me three times to squash down the side so I could get a foothold on the edge, and by that time I had somersaulted over the edge and landed over Mama's pink feet. She just looked down at me and smiled. 'Oh, Bruno! You are so funny sometimes and you make me laugh so much.' And with that she swept down to pick me up and gathered me in her soft warm arms where she scattered sweet-sweet kisses on my baby head and walked with me to the courtyard where my morning papers awaited.

'You are such a good boy, Bruno; you never cause me any stress,' Mama said lovingly. I smiled at myself and felt proud as I walked to my papers and fulfilled my morning duties.

Then Bablu would come for me and my morning gifts for the compost tip and then we would walk around the garden to see if anything new had happened, and by the time we reached the balcony we certainly noticed a new happening.

Baba and Ralph were in a heated argument over what had happened yesterday. 'You are supposed to my friend, Ritchie, yet you didn't defend me and you let her accuse me of such atrocities.'

Ritchie replied, 'Baba, yesterday had nothing to do with me. First I knew of anything was when you shoved me in the car and you took me to that Raju's house.'

'Yes,' shouted Baba, 'but when we came back to the house you could have defended me.'

Ritchie was incredulous, 'But what on earth could I say? The story had been already told by Raju and I had no other story planned.'

BABA AND HIS BUS

Baba started to throw his few tattered belongings into the black bin bag he had acquired from Mama's storage cupboard, but there didn't seem so much in the bin bag. 'I'm going to make my breakfast now,' he said, and Ritchie followed him into the kitchen.

But Bablu had just switched on the fountain in the courtyard and not checked the water pressure so both Baba and Ritchie got showered with sparkly silver water.

With Mama being a sort of an inspirational artist, one day she emptied a packet of silver glitter that made the water look really magical. But not at 9 am in the morning, both of them were covered from head to toe in silver sparkly water and shouting loudly. Ritchie's dog-end that was hanging from his lower lip looking very pretty with its new sparkly dress and Baba's silver suit made him look like an alien from another world.

Perhaps it was the other world that Mama was talking about it the universe world where her friend God lives?

Mama and Bablu were in the kitchen also making breakfast, and when the pair walked in Baba defiantly ignored Mama, who was dressing the luscious red tomatoes on the yellow cutting board while Bablu was chopping the cilantro for the omelette. Mama's eyes were red from crying.

'Oh, my darling, Liz!' Ralph cried as he ran to comfort her with his arms open, 'don't cry love, your son is with you!'

Baba piped up. 'You doddering old fool, Ritchie, you are making a fool of yourself. How can you be her son? You are old enough to be her father!'

'I don't mean me, you insensitive man. Her son is Bruno,' Ritchie replied.

'Oh, don't worry about my crying, dear Ritchie, my tears are from the onions I chopped before,' Mama said happily.

'Oh well, thank goodness for that. I thought you were still crying from last night and I was shocked to see you crying again.'

'No no, my dear friend. Now that has all passed I have only my son by my side and I'm happy, so I'm making a nice breakfast for us all before Baba catches his bus at 1 pm.'

Baba lowered his voice: 'My bus?'

'Yes, your bus,' answered Mama. We all looked at Baba, we just couldn't believe Mama's remark.

'My bus,' he said again, but several octaves higher. 'Since when was I getting a bus at 1 pm? This is news to me. Did you know anything about this?' he remarked to Ritchie. With this Ritchie vigorously shook his head and clouded patches of silver sparkled over the whole kitchen table, including me who was sat next to my divine Mama.

I was happy Ritchie had done this shaking up because I love the sparkling thingamajigs, they were so pretty and they matched the pink thingamajigs on Mama's gown.

'Well, Baba,' said Mama, 'all last night I processed yesterday's event through my mind for hours and hours and my sleep would not come. I watched my son in his new bed and I realised that I could never allow this to happen again. So, I decided to end our relationship amicably.'

What did amicably mean? I thought. I could only think by watching everyone's actions and try to work it out in my little head. But by looking at everyone's face, including Bablu's, I could only presume the situation was not good. No one uttered a word, nobody moved, it was as if time had stood still, when all of a sudden, a large-booted foot came my way. But before it could do me any harm it was miraculously saved by Bablu.

At last, Bablu had the courage to intervene, and he placed a curled fist onto Baba's chin that sent him flying through the kitchen out to the courtyard. Everyone was shocked and Bablu's face with the reality of his action went an ashamed colour of red.

I ran to Mama's skirt to whimper under. She swiftly lifted me up and she told me not to worry – Mama was here to protect me. Mama whispered, 'I vowed last night to myself that nothing would ever happen again and it will never will, my little son.'

'Baba, you can now go from my house. I will never regard you as my friend again. You are nothing but a monster for trying to kick my son in front of my own eyes and if it wasn't for Bablu's swift action you would have succeeded to hurt my son. You are no longer welcome in my house, now go and take your belongings and go.'

Baba had a shocking reply: 'Well, if you tell me to take my belongings, then hand over Bruno to me. I brought him all the way from Gorai, he is mine!'

'You brought him as a gift for me,' Mama said to Baba.

Baba shouted at Mama, 'But straight away you said you didn't like dogs; they were sniffy and smelly.'

'I have changed. That was then this is now,' said Mama. 'Having Bruno has taught me to love all creatures, and Bruno that very night the first night I saw him laying on your dirty cloth by the washing machine made me blindly fall in love with him. From that very moment Bruno was not just a little dog from Gorai but he was my son from the divine, so don't even talk to me anymore or I'll have your belongings thrown on the road.'

With the miracle speech Ritchie pulled Baba from the courtyard floor, leaving a silver shape of Baba's giant form on the marble floor. 'You have overstepped your mark, Baba, even I, your closest, friend am ashamed of your actions. What I have just witnessed is beyond anyone's imagination. I will go home on the bus with you to make sure that you are safe but after that our relationship will finish. I don't want to be associated with you anymore!' said Ritchie.

Ritchie explained to Mama that he would always be there for her, offering his friendship, but was deeply saddened by the behaviour of Baba. But Ritchie knew he must leave as he was falling very much in love with my beautiful Mama.

Within fifteen minutes they had both left the house. Baba with his bin bag and Ritchie with his battered leather briefcase and his morning paper. They arrived in in a rickshaw and left in a rickshaw. The last we saw of them was Ritchie saving his Ralph Lauren baseball cap from falling into a muddy puddle. Just like a comedy act.

Bablu took Mama's hand and gently pulled her away from the huge entrance gate and guided her gently back to the house. He really wanted to pull her tightly into his arms but even as her dearest friend he could never gather the courage to do this. He would make sure that she was safe from harm. So, with me under his other arm we all walked back into the house.

'As bad as all this is, Bablu,' said Mama, 'I'm afraid I still have some sort of feeling for him. I could never imagine him doing something like this. Perhaps I'm too soft, Bablu.'

THE ROYAL PRINCE BRUNO
MEETS CHEEKY CHOPS

So, although in her heart there was a little sadness for Baba, Mama knew that her heart and feelings were never matching. Ritchie and Bablu she felt so safe with, and she felt happy that the divine was there to help her. Ritchie would often come to visit her on the bus and Bablu was a constant friend. Now everything was happy and cheerful and Bruno was growing into a beautiful dog. Everywhere they went people would stop and look at him and ask about his breed, but Mama knew nothing of his true ancestry until one day she was reading the Times of India when she saw an article about old Indian breed of dogs, she read about ten breeds of Indian dogs, including my own.

Mama went on the computer to verify the fact and instantly it showed a picture of a Kombai hound who was identical to me, but not quite as handsome, of course. It needed owners of the same breed to ring them urgently. Apparently, the Kombai hound was extremely rare and was needed for breeding purposes. But unluckily for me my Mama had had me sterilised a month before, because I was becoming somewhat of a playboy and was jumping the six-foot wall and running after the girls.

This was nothing to do about my love for Mama, for I was universally bonded to my Mama. But Mama had to take Dilip the vet's advice on an operation, because I had scraped my tummy and caused dreadful bacterial infection in my body, which was only detected after Mama noticed that blood was creeping from my paws. After five days on drip and antibiotics Dilip did the procedure.

I was kept inside the house for a full week. I didn't feel any different after my operation and Mama said that Dilip had told her it would take at least six months for my body to readjust.

I had no idea what that meant because in those months I acquired a new friend, a lovely black and white mongrel who crept into our mansion on her tummy. Squashing herself through our huge metal gate and even the smaller golden gate, and carried on until Mama saw her.

She was so thin and emaciated Mama took pity on her and spoke to her. 'So what are you doing here, you cheeky girl! You know you don't live here. I can see you are so thin so I can see that you are very hungry, so come into the kitchen.'

I had already smelled her presence and went to inspect the welcome intruder. The cheeky girl was lovely but very thin. Mama told her to come with us to the kitchen where she was breaking a roasted chicken leg into two generous pieces. The larger one she gave to me – Mama loved feeding me by hand – but as soon as the roasted thigh was in my mouth Neena (the girl intruder) immediately reached up on her toes, because she was slightly smaller than me. Her teeth were securely anchored into my chicken thigh where it was gently arrested and transferred into her mouth, so my Mama then gave me a small chicken drumstick.

Mama laughed at the scenario, which was enacted with a hunger plan from our new friend and immediately on this act of unselfishness on my behalf. Mama called her 'Cheeky Chops' instead of Neena. She only lived around the corner so Neena stayed on with us on a bed and breakfast contract. She would stop for four weeks or so and then go home for few days.

This she did very happily for some two years. Mama loved her because she was so funny and I was never jealous about the fact because together the two of us made a good team.

After dinner we were allowed a doggie chewy stick which was white rawhide cow skin. She would come and sit next to Mama on the marble veranda, which I never minded because I would sleep on Mama's sweet pink toes, but if company came to the house Cheeky Chops could proudly walk up and down with the white chewy stick in her mouth at such an angle it would look like a real cigarette. When Cheeky Chops made her entrance she would make everyone laugh at her antics, something no one had witnessed before, and she would saunter along with the dog chewy in her mouth and would greet each and every one with a pet handshake.

Everyone praised Mama for Cheeky Chops' performance but Mama would never accept the compliment as she told everyone that Cheeky Chops belonged to Darrel and Jenette from round the corner.

One sunny summer's day a huge rattling came from the gate. Bablu went running to find Jenette with a huge chain and was shaking it at Bablu. Bablu asked her what she wanted and she shouted back 'I want Neena back, my dog you stole from me.'

Clearly a misunderstanding, Bablu said she only came to play with Bruno. Mama and I heard all the commotion and immediately ran towards the entrance. I ran and sheltered under the beautiful mango tree to survey for myself. It was clear to me that Jenette wanted Cheeky Chops to return. So I ran and galloped towards her with my new black leather collar that Mama had just bought me with shiny metal studs which represented authority. I was now Mama's second security guard. Jenette wasn't frightened by my subdued voice so I turned around and saw Cheeky Chops sitting on the courtyard steps looking rather frightened, so without hesitation I put on my deep masculine howl and ran towards her at fifty miles per hour with my black long velvety ears blowing in the summery breeze. I galloped like a horse in the hunting party with all the power and ferocity of the pack. Jenette was frantically shaking her metal chain, but when she saw me in full power she quickly got the message and frantically ran for her life with the chain dragging behind her.

She shouted to Bablu to bring her back and she would give him two hundred rupees for his trouble.

After the fright of their life, not mine of course, we turned around to see Cheeky Chops wasn't there. Had this been a trick by Jenette and Darrel to get Cheeky Chops back?

We were all stunned and we all ran back in the house shouting her name, but there was no answer. No bark or whimpering. We looked all over the house and back garden area and we almost gave up. Then I found her cowering in the guest room in the corner behind a large suitcase.

We were all so happy to find her she jumped for joy at all of us for her rescue, but this time she kissed everyone. She ran into the kitchen and dove into the drinking bowl and licked and supped it until it was dry. Then she ran around the kitchen, jumping between Mama's and Bablu's legs, finally kissing me on my black dripping nose. I think she was so happy and so were we all! Our little family was completely happy again.

The next morning Cheeky Chops went missing. We all looked for her frantically and then Bablu thought he would take a walk on the road. After five minutes Bablu saw Cheeky Chops on the wall of her house in her usual pose just by the front gate.

She had come back for bed and breakfast to her original owners, to Jenette and Darrel, but for now we only have to guess this and the whim of Cheeky Chops only.

I'll certainly miss her but I'm sure it will be only for a week at the most, as Mama had the best food – beef, chicken liver, roast chicken and roast potatoes – which she said was her favourite dinner. She said she loved the gravy like I do. I remember one day she had licked her plate clean and there was a little left on my plate, so she stood and waited until I had I had almost finished. I love Mama's gravy more than anything – Mama would make the gravy with roast chicken juices and Maggi stock cubes, and it was just like drinking liquid chicken.

I felt sorry for Cheeky Chops and I allowed her to come to share my plate and that little bit of gravy satisfied the two of us; both of us looking forward to next Sunday's dinner!

Sunday came and I went walking to the gate to see my friend. Where on earth could she be? I thought. My little brain was becoming little overactive. I walked as far as I could on the road to see if I could see her but unfortunately only caught sight of a local dog called Bobby. He was a bit of a boy and could only pass the time of the day with you if you were a female, but I tried to chat to him anyhow.

'Bobby! Would you spare me a minute if you can? I need some help!'

Bobby must have been ten or so, for he was brown and white and growing in an irregular length all over his body. I know he was eating or scrapping with the local heroes. He looked like he didn't know about water or of a lick or slob bath. His owners, as they called mummies and daddies in Goa, were very old themselves and would never be more a couple of metres away from one another at any time of the day unless it was Bobby's romancing time. Unfortunately Bobby had no collar only a piece of dirty coconut string which would sometime roll around his neck and slowly stick up his nostril causing one almighty itch and thundering sneeze. His girlfriends never seemed to notice it and his charisma was as warm as the local bull in the weekly bull fight.

'Bobby have you seen Cheeky Chops?'

Bobby replied, 'I wish you would never call her that. Her name is Neena, and she was one of my first girlfriends.'

My heart did a somersault when I heard that remark. Cheeky Chops and I were best of friends, so luckily she wasn't his girlfriend now. I certainly wouldn't be happy about that! In fact, I may have given one almighty blow to the left cheek if the flamingo gate would have not kept us apart – cheeky bugger! Cheeky Chops was only our property and no one else's.

Days and weeks passed and Cheeky Chops was starting to become a distant memory, when all of a sudden, early morning came and a rattle of the bell on the outside wall was heard.

Bablu ran immediately to see what was happening. It was Cheeky Chops with her masters Jenette and Darrel. Cheeky Chops was looking sideways towards her escape through the gate but before she could make a run for it Bablu grabbed my rope. Mama came running down the steps accompanied by me and we were all shocked when we saw the three of them.

Darrel started with a matter-of-fact speech: 'Elizabeth, I myself and my family are moving to Mumbai to be with our children and obviously we have to think about the dogs. It's been decided that we will take the other three dogs with us but we realise that Neena would be happier with you and Bruno. We were a bit harsh on you when we came to bring her home some months ago. We kept her tied up for a month and hoped it would help but it didn't, not for a minute. Her face was unhappy and she barely touched her food. I hope you could help us all. It's better with us being with our children, we are getting on a bit, and for safety reasons she is better with you here in Bastora.'

Both Mama and Bablu looked astonished at this announcement but we were all astutely happy that Cheeky Chops would be back in our family. They untied the chain and Cheeky Chops just laid still with her head on the gravel floor until Jenette tapped her gently on her bottom. Cheeky Chops neither looked right or left, but Jenette's eyes started to trickle thick juicy tears down her powdered face and into the blue polka sports dress.

It was quite obvious that both Darrel and Jenette had some love for Cheeky Chops but perhaps Cheeky Chops never fitted in with the other three dogs and our place was a retreat for her. We went over to meet her. Mama twisted her ears and Bablu stooped over her to talk to her quietly and I rubbed her snout with mine (that's Cheeky Chops of course not Jenette) which means in doggy language 'I missed you, my dear friend'. Slowly she started to raise herself from the ground and put her right foot forwards in order to move. She faltered and stood still, it was as she didn't know what to do, but Bablu stepped forwards to pick her up and I stood on my back legs to see her face. She looked so unhappy, perhaps she will really miss Darrel and Jenette more then she could think, or perhaps she thought that she was being disposed of.

Mama rubbed her noise and kissed her lightly, which I'm sure immediately made Cheeky Chops happy. Slowly she trotted with me to the bottom steps of the veranda where she turned to look at them both Darrel and Jenette, seeing looks of love on their faces.

The tears were still dropping from Jenette, but now furiously and running onto her skirts a voluminous one in the same materiel of her blouse; lakes of darker blue were been mopped up with Darrel's checked handkerchief, while a brand-new dog-end was in Darrel's right hand, smoking away by itself.

'Elizabeth...' said Darrel, 'you know, Neena never belonged to us either. She was a nomad. I was walking home from the samosa shop one evening when I sensed something was by our side. It was Neena with an enchanting smile on her face and she stared intently at the cigarette in my hand, watching the vanishing smoke, and stayed by my side until we reached the garden gate.'

Darrel and Jenette's house looked like navel establishment. Blue and white with a captain's wheel made into a gate with the ship's anchor as a handle – apparently Darrel used to be a ship's captain some years ago.

Neena was so friendly that he decided to let her through the gate, but infuriatingly the other dogs wouldn't allow her so there was fighting all the time, especially at meal times.

'So her coming to you both will be better for her and we would be happy with our children around us. We are both grateful to you for helping us, and I'm sure she will be better in a few days.'

But she wasn't. Cheeky Chops was still subdued, until Mama decided to take her to the vets where Marilyn announced that Cheeky Chops was deeply depressed. She gave her a long silver needle in her hip and a small bottle of homeopathic medicine

Slowly she became Cheeky Chops again and told me her whole story which was so hard for me to understand.

One day when Cheeky Chops was eating her food she said some dogs came over the wall and she fought with them all. They ran as fast as they could but then ended up in another area where we had never been in. They were all still together, but lost and very dehydrated. 'I found your pool so we all crept in there at night time,' she said. The next morning they learnt that all of their little family had been taken away from Goa.

'My heart broke,' Cheeky Chops confided, 'my family had gone, I was all alone.'

'But now you have us all!' I joyfully said. 'We were all miserable when you were taken away, you're part of our family and always will be.'

'One thing to be sure, Bruno, I will never leave this house again. I will never be curious of the world outside,' said Cheeky Chops.

After that scenario of love and joy and anticipation, we were taken in for our Sunday breakfast of scrambled eggs while Darrel and Jenette walked back to their navel house.

We all felt sorry for them, but they were back quicker than we thought with Cheeky Chops' collar and rusty chain, which Mama thanked them for and assured Cheeky Chops she would buy her a nice sparkly pink collar and chain which we would only use on our trips to the beach.

A few days later I noticed Mama crying. 'Whatever is wrong?' asked Bablu.

'Well, it's just I been thinking of you having to leave for Bengal, Bablu. It reminds me of Cheeky Chops – just what am I to do?' Mama said, worried.

'But I have to go madam,' said Bablu. 'The government is giving us our due quotation of land and only heads of family can sign. I swear I will only be away for the shortest time possible. I'll book my seat on the bus.'

Mama thought quickly. 'Go on the plane – we won't be apart for so long then...'

Bablu's eyes started to water. This was the first time madam had uttered anything even along those lines of hidden affection, apart from the time she made him a chocolate cake for his birthday as a surprise that brought tears to his eyes. No one had ever made a cake for him before, let

alone pipe the words, 'Bablu my dearest friend.' It warmed his heart and brought tears to his eyes.

The four of us enjoyed it bit by bit. Me with my little daffodil plate and Bablu and madam with their flowered garden plates that came from Staffordshire in England (the porcelain county). I had a sparkly water and Bablu and Mama had a bottle of local champagne which Mama said was almost as good as her favourite Champagne (Veuve Clicquot). I had never had sparkling water before and got such a shock when bubbles came busting through my nose! Mama thought it was sweet, as I had never experienced this before but I thought differently and insisted to myself never to have those sparkling water again!

The conversation of Bablu leaving continued, 'But what am I going to do with you so far from here?'

'I'll only be away for few months,' he said reassuringly.

Mama replied, as warm tears fell from her eyes, 'But, Bablu, you know the government can take months or even years, I would never be able to cope with it. Let your brother have the title deed, you have more then you ever need, stay and we will be a couple.'

Bablu thought for a moment, could he ask for his mother to send the title deeds by post? This would be impossible, he thought, 'I don't even think that even with lots of wrapping it would get passed to borders of Goa.'

'Bablu, perhaps you can take a lovely shawl when you go to visit her this time when you go to your land registration.' Lovely Mama thinking of others as always.

'Yes, perhaps I'll do that, madam,' Bablu concluded.

Nothing more was said on the subject of Bablu's impending departure.

CLEMENTINE

The days came closer to the outwards journey and Elizabeth was becoming uneasy with the thought Bablu leaving. He packed his bag for the next day.

Even I was uneasy. I knew something was happening and wandered around the garden until I found my little friend the garden fairy, Clementine.

Clementine was named as such because her Mummy had found her under a clementine bush, but she suited the name because she had pale orange hair and lovely orangey cheeks. I was startled when I found her – this was the first garden fairy I had ever seen.

'I'm here to make your garden magical,' said Clementine, 'whenever there is a problem, I will try to help solve it.'

I thought hard, 'Well I don't know if it's a problem or not, but Bablu is returning to Kolkata for some professional business and my mama seems to be dreadfully sad. I think she will miss him badly.'

'Well let me consult my magical flower,' said Clementine. 'It will find a solution to for the problem.'

'How do you know this?' asked Bruno.

'Let me show you,' she said. We both tip toed to the magic marigold patch. Clementine bent over and picked out the largest and freshest marigold of them all.

'Well good morning, Clemmy!' said Mary the marigold.

'Good morning, Mary,' said Clementine.

'I would like to ask you for your magical help,' said Clemmy, 'our mistress is rather distressed of because Bablu is having to leave for short time and it had upset out mistress considerably.'

'Well, tell me your story,' said Mary (she was always said to connect to her friends in the garden, and of course to our mistress's friend God who was always spoken about but never seen, but everyone adores).

'OK,' said Mary, 'let's begin.'

We were told to close our eyes and told to cover our eyes with our hands, in my case it was my paws, which was a bit tricky sitting on my haunches without support of Mama's leg.

Then we had to repeat after her: 'Dear God, today we are asking for your attention for our dear mistress and her friend, Bablu. Please devise some plan that he returns home safely, we will all be eternally grateful and happy. And also will you have a word with Sid the garden slug and his gang – they are destroying all the roots on our babies and it is the most upsetting for us all. Amen.'

All off a sudden a silver cloud drifted and settled all over us, little silver stars settled over our heads and hands and all over my feet, but we all felt blissfully happy.

'The job is done now, Clemmy you can rest assured that everything will be alright,' assured the marigold.

'Thanks so much, Mary,' said Clemmy.

I echoed my one word: Amen. Clementine made us very happy but what can we do to reassure Mama who was desperately miserable. And even my freshly brushed teeth and expertly coffered hair wasn't doing the trick…

I licked her toe and brought her a white daisy and placed it on her silver toe ring – she didn't even notice! I'll not bother in future, I thought.

Oh, what am I saying, she is my beloved Mama. Just how can I even think it? So I went to Clementine for more advice.

Clementine shook her mane of peachy hair and smiled at me. 'Oh, don't worry so much Bruno. God knows our problem and soon it will be solved, but we will try to comfort Mama somehow – I have to think hard. I should never do this, Bruno. And I hope the kingdom of fairies will forgive me… I have to speak to her to give her reassurance and you know we are not allowed to talk to humans, it's the unwritten law of this garden.'

She twinkled herself from the ground and I pivoted onto a nearby jasmine bush, its perfume was divine, and she then looked into the sky and started to sing. The beautiful sound attracted Mama, who ran to the garden to see what was going on.

Clementine fluttered to her shoulder. 'I'm Clementine, we have never meet before but I'm here to help you. The garden and Bruno are all magical and we were all sent out here to help you, every flower and tree in the garden and birds in the garden know about your problem so we are all asking God for his help. He said you are his holy child and while you remain in this magical house nothing bad will happen to you.'

Clementine sat on Mama's shoulder and swung her legs back and forth, wrapping a chain of marigolds around her neck they were all covered in little silvery stars from above. It seemed to Mama that everyone was in on the plan.

The song of happiness wrapped its arms around Mama's heart, when far ahead she noticed Bablu walking towards her with his small leather case that Mama had bought him for his journey. He looked so forlorn.

Immediately she turned and ran back to the house, tears running from her blue eyes.

Clementine in shock flew from her shoulder where Bruno was waiting. 'Oh dear,' she said, 'this is much worst then I imagined…'

Bablu reached the courtyard and grabbed hold of Madam's hand and lovingly pulled her.

'What is it, my darling Elizabeth,' asked Bablu.

Mama's heart warmed. 'That's the first time you have called me darling...'

I was sitting on top of Bablu's suitcase trying with all of my might to make it very heavy for him to lift, but was intently listening to his every word.

'Elizabeth, you have always been my darling, from the very minute I saw you, but I knew my circumstances would never allow you to be in love with me. You were way above my status so the best next thing for me was to be in your presence as much as I could, so when I had the chance to work for you, it felt like Christmas was here. In fact it was Christmas! It was the first Christmas at Piara – it was magical for me,' said Bablu.

It was magical for Mama, who then slipped and fell into Bablu's arms.

They both laughed and Bablu said, 'Perhaps it's the mosquito spray?!'

Mama replied instantly, 'No, I'm delirious with happiness not with shock this time.'

The past year flashed in their minds and all the things that had happened were full of joy, and apart from Baba's episode, full of happiness as well. It just couldn't end now, not now when they had just declared their love for one another.

'Bablu I've just been thinking – don't go to sign for the land in your hometown. Give power of attorney to your brother the land will always be in your family name. You have more than enough here,' proposed Mama.

LOVE IS THE ANSWER

There was no need for anymore words now everything was sorted. Bablu and Mama would now be together for ever and we would be together as one for ever. And now that Mama knows that I can understand everything because of the magical garden we will also be closer than ever.

We went outside again, me under Bablu's arm and holding Bablu's hand. Clementine joined us with the few of her fairy friends. Cheeky chops followed and tried in to pick up the story of the conversation given by God and his magic garden. Every day will be Sunday with all my friends, the fairies and Cheeky Chops for company.

The little brown suitcase had sat all by himself until nighttime, we all felt sorry for him for us forgetting him because now I know through Clementine that everything on the Earth needs caring for and loving. He was such a handsome case with a beautiful brass lock and lovely, neat stitching.

Bablu found a lovely showcase with the shiny glass door on and put him to rest in there where we could talk to him and promise that one day we would take him on a holiday somewhere special. And we named him Edward because he looked so regal sitting on the red velvet cushion.

I sometime think of Mama and Papa in Gorai and wondered how they were, and I thanked Ritchie and Baba in my mind for making my life full of Sundays. My life has been so happy and I thank God for showing me his little white church and the pristine white wafers on the shiny white plate, because I know in my heart this was my gift from God and my years of Sundays. We all are still one magically happy family.

Mama and Bablu, Cheeky Chops and Clementine, and the myriads of little souls from the iridescent dragonfly to the sugar ants we were all created to live as one by God, but only a chosen few were bestowed with the gift of understanding and the gift of love.

Through speech we were truly blessed. This garden was a garden of enchantment and the house was protected with love from everyone!

That night we all gathered outside to watch the full moon. There was no need of a word of love to be spoken. The magic of the moon and the happiness on her face blessed all of us and for that we were eternally grateful. We lit our little candles and thanked the divine for this beautiful life full of love and kindness which extends to the rest of mankind for ever and ever. Amen.

WHERE'S MY WORMS !!

BA-BLU + MA-MA
DECLARING THEIR LOVE

HENRY

MAMA

CLONE

HENRYS CED

CLEMATINE